D1085890

## "LEAD YOUR HORSE!
## THERE'S ICE UNDERFOOT."

Private Malone could barely see Lady Hightower, bent far forward into the wind. The others were lost in the blizzard. Malone hit a patch of ice and felt his boot go out from under him.

He gripped the reins of his bay tightly, and managed to pull himself back onto the trail, gasping. The snow cleared briefly and he saw Lady Hightower, her hands to her mouth, staring at him in unconcealed panic. Then he saw the frantic pawing of the packhorse. The hooves of the horse clattered against the stone and then struck nothing but air as it slid backward and over...

## *EASY COMPANY*

# EASY COMPANY

## AND THE BIG BLIZZARD

JOHN WESLEY
HOWARD

A JOVE BOOK

EASY COMPANY AND THE BIG BLIZZARD

A Jove book / published by arrangement with
the author

PRINTING HISTORY
Jove edition / April 1982

ISBN: 0-515-06032-1

Jove books are published by Jove Publications, Inc.,
200 Madison Avenue, New York, N.Y. 10016. The words
"A JOVE BOOK" and the "J" with sunburst are trademarks
belonging to Jove Publications, Inc.

PRINTED IN THE UNITED STATES OF AMERICA

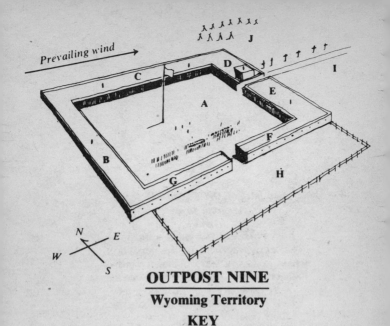

## OUTPOST NINE
### Wyoming Territory
### KEY

**A.** Parade and flagstaff

**B.** Officers' quarters ("officers' country")

**C.** Enlisted men's quarters: barracks, day room, and mess

**D.** Kitchen, quartermaster supplies, ordnance shop, guardhouse

**E.** Suttler's store and other shops, tack room, and smithy

**F.** Stables

**G.** Quarters for dependents and guests; communal kitchen

**H.** Paddock

**I.** Road and telegraph line to regimental headquarters

**J.** Indian camp occupied by transient "friendlies"

INTERIOR                                    OUTSIDE

## OUTPOST NUMBER NINE
### *(DETAIL)*

Outpost Number Nine is a typical High Plains military outpost of the days following the Battle of the Little Big Horn, and is the home of Easy Company. It is not a "fort"; an official fort is the headquarters of a regiment. However, it resembles a fort in its construction.

The birdseye view shows the general layout and orientation of Outpost Number Nine; features are explained in the Key.

The detail shows a cross-section through the outpost's double walls, which ingeniously combine the functions of fortification and shelter.

The walls are constructed of sod, dug from the prairie on which Outpost Number Nine stands, and are sturdy enough to withstand an assault by anything less than artillery. The roof is of log beams covered by planking, tarpaper, and a top layer of sod. It also provides a parapet from which the outpost's defenders can fire down on an attacking force.

# one ───────────────

Private Trueblood reached the end of the parapet along the stockade wall of Outpost Number Nine, and turned and yawned, glancing at the eastern sky to see that finally the horizon was lightening, that his night of cold, monotonous guard duty was nearly ended.

Trueblood yawned again and marched slowly back toward the gate where he had met Yount countless times that night as they turned around to walk the parapet again, like mechanical bears in a shooting gallery. The plains became slate gray, emerging from the darkness of night to take on form and substance.

A lamp flickered on in the barracks. That would be Reb McBride, the bugler, who was first up as a rule. Inside half an hour, Reb would be blowing sweet reveille and not long after that, the even sweeter grub call.

Trueblood glanced toward the mess hall and saw the smoke rising from the stovepipes to merge with the dull gray sky, and his stomach gurgled with anticipation. All

1

Trueblood wanted was a warm breakfast and a day's sleep.

He turned again and walked back toward the gate, holding himself a little more erect now that Captain Conway and First Sergeant Cohen were likely to be up and stirring, and glanced at the northern skies to his right.

He frowned and wiped his raw eyes. The sky was a deep, deep blue, almost blue-black to the north and northwest. It was an eerie, almost electric blue, of the shade they called Prussian.

He stared at it a moment, with interest, until he made his turn and the more compelling thoughts of breakfast and sleep returned to sweep away what he imagined to be a trick of sunrise.

McBride emerged from the enlisted barracks and blew reveille, setting the yawning, stretching outpost into a sluggish motion.

Armstrong and MacArthur staggered toward the gate, reported to Wilson, who was corporal of the guard that morning, and relieved Trueblood and Yount, who clambered down the ladders from the parapet and returned to the barracks.

McBride had come out without his greatcoat. The days had been growing warmer lately, and he figured there was no need for such clothing. Now, following Trueblood and Yount back toward the barracks, he began to shiver. It was still damned cold, he decided. Or maybe he was getting older, the circulation slowing. Before grub call, he snatched up his greatcoat. He was glad he had; it was no warmer then, half an hour later, with the yellow ball of the sun cresting the low, dark horizon.

In the transient Indian camp to the northeast of Outpost Number Nine, Windy Mandalian strode from the tipi he had shared with Running Doe. The woman still slept, snuggled in the warmth of her buffalo skins and furs, drugged by a night of lovemaking.

The scout was not one for sleeping in, however; first

light arrived an hour after Windy had risen.

Drinking hot coffee by starlight, he felt it in the air. Dawn confirmed his suspicions. A blue wall moved slowly southward toward Wyoming, and Windy turned and picked up his buffalo coat and badgerskin gloves before riding his appaloosa pony to Number Nine.


She opened a sleepy eye and looked up at her man. Tall, handsome, silhouetted by the faint light that filtered through the curtained window.

"I'll be up in a minute," Flora Conway yawned. "I'm sorry, I should have been up by now. I don't know why I'm so tired."

"Don't you?" Captain Warner Conway finished buttoning his tunic and returned to the bed. He sat beside his wife, enjoying the picture she presented—sleep-tousled dark hair, yawning mouth, nightdress unbuttoned still, hinting at the smooth swell of her breasts.

Flora leaned forward and drew his head to her breasts, kissing his forehead as she smoothed his dark hair with a gentle hand.

"Cold, isn't it?" Flora asked. "Or is it me?"

"It's chilly," the captain agreed. He felt her fingers running down the nape of his neck and he felt the stirring between his thighs.

Flora's arms encircled him and she whispered into his ear, "What time is it?"

"Why?" He glanced at his pocket watch. "There's not *that* much time." He kissed her lips and nuzzled her sleep-warmed throat.

"It wouldn't take long. Not this morning, Warner."

"I really don't think—"

Flora had begun unbuttoning her nightdress, a teasing smile playing on her lips.

"Flora..." he protested, but that was as far as his protest went. She shrugged out of her nightdress; her smooth shoulders and still-firm breasts were bared, drawing the captain's eyes, hands, lips.

3

"I'll be late," he complained. Already he was removing his tunic, however.

"There has to be some advantage in being commanding officer, Warner."

"There is," Conway said, slipping out of his pants and into bed. "I'm the man who has the privilege of sleeping with the CO's lady."

"They won't miss you for ten minutes," Flora murmured.

She had shed her nightdress, slipping from its sheer cocoon. Now his lean, hard body was against her, and she breathed with slow contentment as his lips surveyed her breasts with slow, lingering kisses.

She reached between his legs and cradled his swelling erection. She threw back the bedsheets as he got to his knees and let his lips run across her abdomen.

She clutched him more tightly now, spreading her legs as his kisses reached her inner thighs, sending tremors through her body, pinpoints of electrical current that ran from her crotch to her breasts, causing her nipples to tingle.

Her thighs parted and Warner's fingers explored the familiar, compelling warmth of Flora's inner flesh. Her scent too was familiar, but always intriguingly new. The button of flesh that lay nearly concealed in the soft, curly hair that flourished there was rigid, and Conway's fingers ran along it, tracing ovals, and Flora shuddered, lifting her pelvis.

Her fingers ran along the length of his shaft, pausing at the head of it to move around it in maddeningly slow circles. Flora rolled toward him, her smile deep, her eyes bright, and Warner Conway lay back, placing his head on the pillow.

"What is it?" he asked.

"Nothing. Nothing. Lie back, dear. I know exactly what I want and exactly how to find it."

"In ten minutes?" he asked with a mock frown.

"Damned near in ten seconds." He lay back and she

straddled him, still holding his erection. "The way you've got me excited, you brute." Her voice was low and breathy now.

Conway cupped her breasts. Her hair, falling free, lay across his chest as she bent forward to kiss him. Then Flora shook back her hair and lifted herself, touching the head of his erection to her crotch.

Conway's hands joined her there. He spread her gently, feeling her fingers, now moist with her own juices, and his sex, which pulsed and wriggled with need. Together, their fingers interlaced, they eased his shaft into her depths. Slowly she settled on him, slowly, her inner muscles rippling against him.

Conway's hands still rested there and his thumbs found her clitoris, moving in slow circles around it as Flora, sitting absolutely still for a moment, tilted her head back. Her eyes were closed, her throat muscles taut with sensual concentration. Her body pulsed against his and gradually she began to sway, to stroke against him.

Warner's hands slipped behind his wife's legs, crawling up the backs of her thighs to run across the soft curve of her buttocks. His finger traced the line of her cleft from the tail of her spine to where he entered her, his finger lingering there to touch the incredible softness of her, to feel her shuddering against him, encircling him.

She had begun to move differently now, to pitch against him, her pelvis grazing his. Her breasts swayed and her thighs quivered with the advent of a soft, utterly pleasurable climax.

He was huge inside her, filling her with joy, with need, and Flora murmured something nonsensical as she moved her hips in tight, demanding circles.

Warner clenched her buttocks tightly, lifting his own hips higher, harder, thrusting against her. Flora gave a little gasp and collapsed against him, kissing his ears, his throat, his chest as Conway, holding her against himself, worked toward his own draining climax.

She was soft and her lips were tender, her body de-

5

manding, and he folded his arms around her, coming with a sudden rush, deeply, passionately.

She lay against him and his hands ran down her smooth, narrow back, across the rise of her buttocks, returning to her shoulders. He held her head by the neck and kissed her hotly.

"Again?" she asked, her finger running along his lips.

"My God, woman—some people are never satisfied!"

"I'm satisfied as long as I have you, Warner. But then, it doesn't hurt to ask, does it? We need a vacation." She rolled away, stretching. Her breasts rose with the motion. "We could spend all day in bed, like newlyweds. Remember Denver?"

"I can't get away, Flora. Maybe next summer."

"Oh, I know it." She yawned, then, with a determined nod, swung her feet to the floor. "But I like to daydream, to pretend." She sat beside him, her hand on his shoulder. She kissed his back and leaned her head against him.

Corporal McBride blew grub call, and Warner Conway came to his feet. He was a methodical man, a soldier, punctual and practical, hardly a daydreamer. She kissed him again and sat watching as he dressed hurriedly.

"Breakfast?"

"I'll eat in Dutch's mess this morning," Warner said. "It *is* cold," he said, frowning. Conway opened the door to the black iron stove that sat in the center of the room, and poked some fresh fuel in—real wood, not buffalo chips. A privilege of rank.

Flora was in her robe now and she came to him, pecking him goodbye. She wanted to hold him, to cling to him, but over the years she had learned not to do so at moments like this.

There was duty, a clock on the wall, his men to care for. She stood beside the door as he went out, striding down the boardwalk toward the kitchen of Dutch Rothausen. Flora stood there until she could no longer see her man. Then, clutching her wrapper to her throat against the cold, she turned and went back into her quarters.

6

Acting Master Sergeant Ben Cohen, the first shirt of Outpost Number Nine, had the coffee going before Captain Conway had arrived at headquarters.

He snapped the captain a salute and blinked as the door to the office was banged shut by the rising wind. "Getting set to blow, is it, sir?"

"It looks like it, Sergeant." The captain, Ben noticed, had a somewhat distracted expression this morning.

"Feels funny out there, I noticed," Cohen said. "Makes the hair on your neck stand up." He poured coffee for his commanding officer and followed him into his office, carrying the opened mail, which he placed at Conway's left hand.

After leaving the captain's office, Sergeant Cohen poured himself a cup of coffee, stoked up the fire, rubbed his arms, and sat at his desk.

No sooner had he seated himself than the door, aided by the gusting wind, burst open and a grizzled, hulking man in buckskins and a buffalo-hide coat appeared.

Cohen glanced up without expression.

"Help you, sir?"

"You can indeed. I hope so, at least. Name's Cambridge," the big man said, without offering a hand. He closed the door behind him and tramped to Cohen's desk. Cambridge had a lean face, bulky shoulders, and a distinctive odor.

"I want to see the commanding officer," he said.

"He's in. I'll ask," Ben said. He wrinkled his nose and went to the captain's door. Rapping once, he entered.

"Man to see you, sir. Buffalo hunter, by the smell of him."

Captain Conway nodded, placed his mail aside, and stood to greet the civilian, who carried a rifle in the crook of his arm. As Ben had warned him, he had a ripe, distinctive aroma about his person.

"Warner Conway," the captain said, extending a hand.

"Cambridge." The buffalo hunter managed to unwind

7

his hand from his Spencer rifle and shake hands. It seemed to be an unaccustomed civility with the man.

"Sit down, tell me what I can do for you."

"I don't need to sit. This is an emergency, Captain. I got a man bad hurt and I need to borry your doctor."

"We do not have a post surgeon, Mr. Cambridge," Conway had to tell him.

"The hell! No doctor on an army post!" Cambridge frowned in disbelief.

"I'm afraid we don't rate one, Mr. Cambridge."

"Christ!" Cambridge sagged into a chair. "The kid's gonna die, looks like," he said, as if speaking to himself.

"What happened?" Conway wanted to know.

Cambridge waved a hand and sighed with disgust. "We hired on a new skinner. Me and Bob Evers, that is. Just a kid he is, name of Harry Daley—not that it matters."

The buffalo hunter leaned forward and explained what had happened.

"Me and Bob Evers had us three skinners—Injuns. But one took off to make medicine, so we took on a green kid off a wagon train. Name of Daley. His folks was going on to Oregon, but they was some squabble—believe the old man wasn't his real daddy, I don't know." Cambridge shrugged. "He wanted to work and we took him on."

Conway had a nearly overwhelming impulse to get up and open the window, Cambridge was that ripe, but he overcame the urge.

Cambridge got on with his tale. "Thing that happened was the kid got careless. He was skinning out a big bull—and I mean a *big* son of a bitch, Captain. Put his knife to that damned bull's gullet and up he rose."

"The bull was alive?"

"He was that," Cambridge confirmed with a nod. "It happens. Evers just thunked the buff across the skull with his shot, you see. Bull went down, out colder than a mackerel, but hardly hurt. It's a skinner's lookout, but the kid was green. The experienced man will give 'em a good kick, make damned sure they're dead and not just down. But Daley, he got to his knees and stuck the bull, and the old buff came to his feet madder'n hornets. Daley jumped up yellin', but he was too slow. Time I unlimbered my rifle and put the bull down for keeps, he'd half tore the kid's leg off."

Cambridge took a deep, tense breath. "It's a bad one, Captain. Thigh bone's all busted up, meat torn away. We got him trussed up and filled with whiskey to numb him some, but the kid's gonna die if the leg don't come off. Me and Bob, neither of us wanted to go after that leg with a skinnin' knife. Likely kill him our own selves. So I rode up here. Bob says, 'Ever' army post has to have a surgeon. It's in the rules.'" Cambridge shook his head. "But I guess it ain't so. You ain't got a doctor, you cain't help us. I'll be going back."

The buffalo hunter rose heavily, his chair scraping on the floor. Conway stood also.

"I said we didn't have a doctor," Conway said, "but I didn't tell you we couldn't help. You hold on. I've got a man who can see to that leg."

Dutch Rothausen mopped his forehead with the back of his hand. Breakfast was over, but dinner was already being prepared. The KPs clattered the dishes together in the dish tubs, and the kitchen filled with steam. A dish slipped and broke against the floor.

Rothausen turned, his red face growing redder, and hollered at the guilty KP. Farnsworth, Dutch's assistant, was burning the beans, and Rothausen bellowed.

"Farnsworth, you fuckhead! Pour some water in these beans!"

Farnsworth appeared, trembling, and ducked away. Pots clattered against the floor. Rothausen looked to the heavens, his eyes rolled back.

Those beans had an awful smell to them. He turned around, frowning, and then saw the man dressed in a buffalo-skin coat, standing in the kitchen door.

"You Rothausen?"

"I am." Dutch ambled to where the buffalo hunter stood. A big man himself, the hunter was dwarfed by Dutch's bulk. "If it's coffee you want, help yourself."

"Captain says I should see you. We need a leg taken off a man, down twenty miles south. Captain says you're the man for the job."

Dutch nodded. It was no new request. He estimated he had taken off more limbs than an average doctor would in ten years of practice. It was a skill born of necessity. "I'll be right with you," Dutch said.

He collected his meat saw, two large butcher knives, and a sharpening steel. Snatching a bottle of brandy from the cupboard, he shouted to his assistant, "I'm leaving, Farnsworth. Should be back by supper."

"All right, Sergeant," Farnsworth said, not bothering to conceal the smile of relief on his face. Dutch could be intimidating with his bulk and low boiling point, and Farnsworth was intimidated.

Dutch stripped off his apron and stuffed it into the burlap sack at his feet, along with the implements and brandy. He watched Farnsworth spill water into the fire, and grumbled. He hadn't had a decent assistant since Torkleson left. "Don't burn the place down!" he shouted.

Then, grabbing his coat and hat, hefting his sack, Dutch joined Cambridge.

Second Lieutenant Taylor hunched his back against the rising wind. He had seen the skies at dawning and had not liked what he saw. Fortunately they were nearly at the perimeter, because, unless Taylor missed his guess, it was going to snow, and snow hard. With luck, however, they would be back at the outpost before it started.

Corporal Miller angled his bay toward Taylor. The three soldiers with him were buffeted by the rising wind, which turned their hatbrims back, lifted their coattails, and whipped the manes of their horses.

"Nothing, sir," Miller reported.

"Thank God." He nodded toward the northern skies. "We don't need any hostile contact now."

"If that's going to be as bad as it looks now, the Indians will be holed up," Miller guessed.

"That's just what *I* have in mind, Corporal."

Miller smiled. His ears were cold and his nose glowed. He looked out across the vast grasslands to the south and east. "What in God's name do they come here for?" he asked.

He referred to the settlers—or would-be settlers. At this time of the year, looking forward to a winter crossing of the Rockies, a few always turned north, off the Bozeman, with the idea of finding a patch of grass to farm.

Little Jack had been prowling this area until recently, and the renegade Arapaho was having a field day. Plenty fancy ribbons, plenty horses—plenty dead settlers.

Taylor answered, "I guess they're looking for something. What does any man come West looking for?"

"If they knew what it was like—really like—there wouldn't be many of them," Miller said.

Privates Dobbs, Forrester, and Burns had arrived. They sat their horses, backsides to the wind, looking expectantly, hopefully to their officer.

"Let's get on back," Taylor said.

"None too soon," Dobbs said. "It's gonna snow like hell, sir."

Taylor agreed with Dobbs's observation. He had already swung his bay's head, and was already pleasantly anticipating a glass of brandy, a cup of coffee, and a warm stove, when he saw them.

"What is that, Miller?"

Miller's eyes followed the lieutenant's pointing, wavering finger. Miller squinted into the distance and saw them for himself.

A black, tiny form rolling northward across the plains, another smaller form beside it. "Looks like a man leading an ox wagon, sir."

11

Dobbs swallowed a curse. That meant they were going to be a while getting to Number Nine. Taylor sighed. "Let's welcome them to Wyoming," he said, glancing again at the northern skies, where the wall of unnatural blue still progressed southward. A granddaddy of a blue norther was fixing to blow, and they couldn't be in a worse position, exposed as they were.

Taylor buttoned the top button on his greatcoat and turned his collar to the wind. They rode southward then, toward the tiny, distant wagon and the incredibly small figure of a man who walked beside it.

Behind them, the massive wall of weather mounted ominously higher and darker; the grass before them trembled in the wind.

Before they reached the wagon, the first snow had begun to fall.

# two ─────────────────────────

    Far to the south and east, Fort Laramie basked in sunshine. Outside the sutler's store there was a plank bench, and there, arms crossed, hat tilted forward over his eyes, a soldier dozed in the morning sun.

    He heard their feet on the plank walk and then was aware of a shadow falling over him. He did not look up, but he heard them well enough.

    "That's him," a cultured male voice said.

    "This one?" the woman's voice was positively aghast.

    "I'm afraid so. Private Malone."

    Malone didn't bother to look up even then. Whatever they were selling, he wasn't buying. He had three days of a two-week furlough left to him. The first eleven days he had spent in Denver trying to raise the dead, and damned near succeeding. He had done enough drinking and enough women to make him believe that it was—as some said—possible to get tired of both.

    Denver had been a whirl of whiskey, roulette wheels,

lace and legs, dance halls and knuckle fighting. Malone figured he needed at least three days to recuperate, and he had started his recuperation program on that sun-warmed bench at Fort Laramie.

"Wake him up," the woman commanded. There was a pause.

"He's bound to wake up by himself sooner or later," a second man's voice suggested cautiously.

"Oh, Charles," she said in exasperation. "What's the matter, do you think he will strike you?" Malone felt something like a stick tapped impatiently against his knee. "Here now, Private Malone, wake up."

The last woman who had said that to Malone had said it with a good deal more finesse, he recollected, and she had gotten better results.

Nevertheless, he tilted his hat back and peered up at them.

There was three of them, all civilians. The bulky man in the long dark coat wore huge flowing mustaches and a top hat. Some sort of sash ran diagonally across his massive, rounded chest. He gazed at Malone as if the soldier were a zoo exhibit.

The second man was narrow in the face, narrow in the shoulders and hips. In his early twenties, he had a narrow mustache under a hooked nose, haughty blue eyes beneath wildly arched brows.

Then there was the woman.

Of moderate height, she had a beautiful, creamy complexion, dark, dark blue eyes, and full, slightly curved lips. Her impressive breasts were concealed but not denied by the elegant blue gown she wore. She carried a parasol over her shoulder, and she twirled it now, impatiently, as Malone squinted into the sun at them.

"Somethin' I can do for you?" Malone drawled. He still had his arms folded on his chest, and now he closed his eyes again. The sun was warm and there was still a dull throbbing behind his eyes from the eleven-day party.

"God, the man doesn't even come to his feet." The

voice belonged to the younger man, and had a heavy British accent. He tapped Malone's boots with a walking stick, and Malone opened an eye halfway.

"Lady Hightower," the older man said, "perhaps..." His voice trailed off as if he had run out of wind. The lady had silenced him by merely lifting an aristocratic eyebrow.

"We must speak with you, Private Malone," Lady Hightower said with infinite patience.

"Go ahead," he replied. "You already woke me up."

"Is this a typical American soldier?" the younger man said in disbelief. "Sir! Private Malone. This is Lady Hightower!"

Malone lifted his hat an inch off his head and muttered, "Pleased."

"You could at least come to your feet." Again he tapped Malone's outstretched boots with his walking stick.

"You do that again and I'll damned sure come to my feet. I'll take that little stick and stick it up your nose for you."

"The nerve!"

"Damn..." the fat man breathed.

"You don't seem to understand—" she began.

"I understand," Malone said, sitting up straight now. "You came along, woke me up, prodded me, and now you want me to come to respectful attention."

He rubbed his jaw and told them, "I'm an American soldier, all right. Thing is, I don't see no American army uniforms on any of you, and much as I'd like to, I just ain't got the time to take orders from every whosit and whatsit that happens by. If you'll excuse me..." Malone leaned back again.

"Sir, your effrontery is intolerable!" the big man sputtered.

"Could be," Malone answered.

"Damn your eyes!" The kid was determined to impress the lady, it seemed. Fortunately she stopped him from

15

taking that downward swing with his walking stick.

"Please, David, I'll handle this," she said. "Mr. Malone"—her voice had dropped to a lower tone, but the strain was telling—"I have spoken to Colonel Haversham, the post commander. He has informed me that you are traveling back to your Outpost Number Nine. Since we wish to travel in that direction, the colonel has assured me that you would, as a matter of courtesy, be happy to act as guide for our party."

"He did, did he?"

"If you do not wish to escort us, I'm sure the colonel would like to be informed of that, and of the reason you choose to refuse."

"I'd be happy to tell him, ma'am. And I'll tell you now. I'm on furlough. That means I'm my own man, not the army's. Second thing is, I don't like being approached so high and mighty. Maybe you've got servants and all in England, or wherever it is you come from, that bob up and scrinch around whenever you snap your fingers. Well, that's all right, I expect. You pay them. You don't pay me."

"Scrinch?" the big man said, his brow furrowing.

"I do understand your sensitivity," Lady Hightower answered. She flashed him a practiced, cold smile. "Is that what I should tell the colonel—that you find us offensive?"

"Tell the old man whatever the hell you like," Malone said. With that, he closed his eyes and dozed. After a minute he heard them walking away; it was the first time he could ever recall hearing footsteps that sounded huffy.

Satisfied with himself, he smiled and let the sun warm him as his dreams rambled through images of young dancing girls, curtained hotel rooms, warm Denver nights.

He came out of it suddenly. A master sergeant and a huge lance corporal had him under the arms and they lifted him roughly to his feet. He was marched down the boardwalk, across the parade, and into the office of Colonel Haversham, where he was aired out, riddled, reamed, and perforated.

After Malone had a full understanding of his own desire to be a goodwill ambassador for the army and to serve the foreign visitors to Wyoming in any way possible, he was let off—mangled, chewed up, but whole.

They were waiting outside, the woman in a dark traveling dress, the men in white dusters. They glanced up at Malone, who muttered:

"Changed my mind."

Sullenly, he retrieved his horse from the post paddock and saddled it, tying down his bedroll and supplies. When he rejoined the three Britishers, they were mounted on their own horses, the lady sitting sidesaddle on a leggy roan.

The younger man, the one the colonel had identified as Dr. David Chapel, a naturalist, was smiling insufferably. Malone looked him in the eye, spat on the ground, and kneed his horse forward.

They left Fort Laramie on the eleventh day of Malone's two-week furlough: a soldier, a naturalist, a trophy hunter—Charles Whittington, third earl of something— and Lady Elizabeth Hightower, an artist. Six pack animals trailed out behind them, carrying guns, tents, camp stoves, canvases and paints, and scientific instruments.

The day was clear, the wind brisk from the northeast, Malone's mood sullen. His head throbbed and his eyes burned.

"I am truly pleased that you did change your mind," Lady Hightower said with that automatic, meaningless smile. "We have been told that this can be rough country."

"Mighty rough, ma'am. Mighty rough."

"I know you're not pleased with our company, Private Malone, but why not make the best of it?"

"I intend to, ma'am." Malone's tone was enigmatic. After a minute he asked, "Just what are you people doing out here unescorted? No scouts, no protection."

17

"Protection?"

"We do have hostile Indians, ma'am."

"Oh." She shrugged. Not having ever seen hostiles, they seemed to have no reality for her. "It's a grand adventure being out here." She waved a hand around her, indicating the plains, the mountains. "You must love it."

"No, ma'am." Malone shook his head. "It's dirty, cold, lonesome, and downright hazardous."

"It's all in the eyes that view the wilderness," Lady Hightower said effusively. "To me, it's a wonderland. Each mile we ride, every direction I look—grandeur! I could paint for a lifetime out here."

"Yes, ma'am."

"You're wasting your breath, Elizabeth," Chapel said. "A soldier sees Indians as enemies, landscapes as battle-grounds. Isn't that right, Private?"

"Mostly," Malone agreed. "Helps to keep a man alive."

"Yes." Chapel smiled indulgently. "By the way, has Lady Hightower mentioned that we wish to traverse the mountains?"

"The mountains!" Malone didn't quite laugh out loud, but he came as close to it as a man can.

Chapel frowned at the disparaging tone of Malone's voice. He explained, "There is a species of scrub cedar I'm especially interested in examining. The earl is still looking for a mountain sheep trophy, and of course there could hardly be a more inspiring terrain for Lady Hightower."

Malone had been shaking his head steadily. Now he glanced at the narrow face of David Chapel.

"Mister, those ain't anthills. That's the Medicine Bow range up there. That peak," he lifted a finger, "is Medicine Bow Peak. That's twelve thousand feet up, Mr. Chapel."

"We certainly weren't planning on scaling the highest peak, Malone," Chapel replied with a dry chuckle. He

18

shared an amused look with Whittington. The big man tugged at his mustache and spoke up.

"See here, there must be passes through the range. Hate to come this near and be denied."

"Sir, that's bad country. Even in the best of times. We got winter coming on. If we get hit with a snowstorm, we'll have the devil's own time getting out of there alive."

"Surely you exaggerate, Malone." Chapel looked to the skies. "And snow! I hardly think so. It's clear as a bell."

"It's clear as a bell to me that you're crazy if you mean to try those high passes this time of year. I won't be a part of it," Malone said flatly.

"We'll discuss it later," Lady Hightower said, wisely stepping in.

Angrily, Chapel turned his horse aside, and he and the earl rode fifty feet apart from Malone and the lady.

"How have you been getting around?" Malone asked.

"Quite simply." She smiled. There was still no warmth in it, and if it was intended to melt Malone, it failed. "The War Department has instructed field personnel to give us whatever assistance we require. It does have advantages—position, I mean."

"I reckon so. So you travel the West with an army escort. Mr. Chapel sticking butterflies, the third earl taking trophies, and you . . . doing whatever you do."

"I am an artist, Private Malone," she said, as if explaining to a child. "I prefer to work in oils, but it is impractical out here. Chiefly I sketch, with an occasional watercolor. This is a broad, beautiful, changing land. I want to record some of it before it has changed for the worse."

"You want to paint Outpost Number Nine?" Malone asked in disbelief.

Lady Hightower laughed aloud at that. Chapel turned in his saddle to glare at them. "Not exactly," she said. "Although I may, who knows?"

She explained, "I'm simply compiling an album of Western life. I've done Indians, ranchers, wildlife. Why not an army outpost?" she asked, inclining her head, measuring the thought.

"You ain't seen it," Malone commented dryly.

"No. But it is on our route. We intend to traverse Wyoming and Montana. From there we shall travel through the northwest Canadian provinces and eventually meet our ship in Vancouver."

"Sounds enchanting," Malone said with hostility.

"You don't approve."

"It's foolish, ma'am. I don't know how you got this far on your own, I truly don't. But from here—"

The boom of a rifle rolled across the plains. The shot seemed to be just beside Malone's ear. His head thundered with the echo. A cloud of black smoke drifted over their horses and was dissipated by the wind.

Charles Whittington sat in his saddle, a rifle at his shoulder. It was a big double rifle, firing at least a .60-caliber bullet. The man was pleased with himself, and Malone, following his eyes, saw a bull elk stretched out dead against the long grass, nearly fifteen hundred feet away.

"Not bad, eh, Private Malone? At that range, from horseback!"

The man was positively glowing. He ejected the spent cartridge. Lady Hightower leaned toward Malone and said, "He's a magnificent shot—you can see why Charles has no fear of red Indians."

"I hope he don't, ma'am," Malone said sullenly. "Because if there's any red Indians around, they damn sure know we're in the area now, don't they?"

She made no answer, and Malone rode away from her, watching as Whittington examined his elk. "Take the rack for me, please, Private," the big man said, turning around.

Malone spat and wheeled his horse around, riding ahead without looking back. Charles Whittington, bemused, stood with his hands on his hips, staring after Malone.

"What's wrong with our guide?" he asked Chapel. "I even said 'please.'" Shaking his head, he stepped back into the saddle, leaving his trophy antlers behind. There would be other elk. "Damned Americans," he murmured, sliding his rifle into its saddle boot. "A puzzling breed."

"Well, maybe he won't be with us much longer, Charles," Chapel said.

"What? Is he deserting us?"

"I don't know. What will he do, do you suppose, when we inform him that we intend to take the mountain route whether Private Malone likes it or not?"

"Oh, I see what you mean." Charles Whittington, Third Earl of Whitechapel, tugged at his long mustaches. "But really, David—to travel with no menial whatsoever!" The earl plainly found the idea appalling.

"If he does quit us. I assure you he will be made to regret it. We have carte blanche from the War Department, and although quitting us may take Malone to his outpost before us, he will have to reckon with us upon our arrival."

Confidently, Dr. David Chapel added, "His commanding officer will have plenty to say to Private Malone, I assure you."


Captain Conway had other things on his mind just then. The snow had begun to fall, not heavily, but with no prospect of letting up. The wind had risen, and several stovepipes had been toppled. One was in the captain's quarters, where water and soot had ruined Flora's red settee and the captain's dinner.

Farnsworth had nearly burned down the kitchen. Dutch was gone on a medical mission. Taylor was far afield, although presumably en route to the outpost.

And now this.

"You know how ugly things can get, sir," Butler said with a slight tremor in his voice.

21

"I do, indeed. Sixteen months back we had a near riot when the beef shipment failed to arrive at your agency on schedule."

"So I've been told. I wasn't there at the time, of course." Butler, a young, blond-haired man with a nervous tic for a smile, turned his hat in his hands.

"How long overdue are they?"

"Childes—the trail boss—put his arrival at anytime between the fourteenth and the eighteenth."

Conway frowned. It was the twenty-second. The herd for the agency beef supplies was being driven up the Texas Trail from Cheyenne. Knowing from past experience that such herds were usually given into the hands of a skeleton crew, Conway could appreciate the agency's concern.

The weather was turning nasty, and if it kept up, the herd might very well bog down or be forced to turn back. Normally, a few Indians could be shaken loose for the job, but Butler had informed Conway that the agency was presently overwhelmed by a measles outbreak—another gift to the red man from his white benefactors.

"Can we count on your assistance, sir?" Butler asked hopefully.

"I don't see that I have much choice," Conway replied. Perhaps the agency Indians were not his direct responsibility. But any dissatisfaction caused by the failure of the beef supplier to deliver could damn sure turn into something he did have direct responsibility for—and quickly.

"I'll send a patrol out to help the drovers through," Conway promised. Butler left, mopping his forehead—another of his nervous habits, even in this bitter cold.

Ben Cohen was wearing his topcoat, although his stove was blazing away merrily. He glanced at the captain.

"Send for Sergeant Olsen, please, Ben. And maybe you'd better have Windy come and see me."

"Trouble at the agency?"

22

Conway explained briefly. Then he went to the window, watching as the snow sifted ceaselessly down. The parade was already a foot deep, tracked across by men and horses.

Windy Mandalian was the first to arrive, and Conway sat him down in his office. "We might have a lost cattle herd down the trail, Windy. I want you and Gus Olsen to take a look and see if you can bring them through to the agency."

The scout simply nodded. Neither man mentioned the deteriorating weather. When Olsen arrived, Conway briefed him, and asked him to find three men who had experience pushing cattle.

"Cattle. There's McBride, of course. Reb's done his time behind a cow. Malone isn't back, I suppose?" Olsen asked.

"No, and I don't expect him in time for this."

"I'll see who else we have, sir," Olsen said, rising.

Conway escorted the noncom to the door. Opening it, they were met by a bitterly cold gust of wind. A few snowflakes drifted into the room to melt against the floor.

Olsen glanced at the captian, shook his head, and left. It took Windy to say it.

"It's a bad one, Captain. Bad." He spat and turned up his collar. "And it's gonna get one hell of a lot worse."

## three ─────────────────

He emerged from the storm like an approaching specter, moving slowly, appearing and disappearing behind veils of wind-shifted snow, the heads of his oxen bobbing wearily.

Cole Littlefield halted abruptly and started to reach for his shotgun, which rested in the box of the wagon, before he recognized that the men wore uniforms of the United States Army.

"Thank the Lord," he sighed, halting his oxen. He stood there, a heavy man in a ragged coat and torn flop hat. Taylor stepped down and spoke to him above the wind noise.

"Second Lieutenant Taylor, sir."

"Cole Littlefield, Lieutenant," the big man answered. "Almighty glad to see you. Almighty glad. I got my wife and little girl with me. Lookin' for a place to nest."

"You turned off the Bozeman?"

"Yes, sir. Didn't think we could make the mountains.

25

Supplies are out, and Mama's in bad enough shape."

"Hurt?"

Taylor stepped down and walked to the back of the wagon. Littlefield threw back the flap to reveal his wife and little girl, wrapped in blankets, huddled against the sideboard.

"No, sir, not sick." Littlefield nodded.

"I see." Taylor nodded. Even the layers of blankets could not conceal the woman's advanced pregnancy. "No, she wouldn't have made the mountain trail. But out here." Taylor waved an arm. "Alone. God, man, there's renegades attacking wagons. Hard weather."

"There's simply times a man has no choice, Lieutenant. This was one of them times. Whatever I found, I figure it'd be better than what I left behind."

Taylor only nodded. Littlefield's observation only held if he considered being scalped, starved, or frozen to death on the plains preferable to whatever life he had left behind.

"We'll take you through to Outpost Number Nine. It's thirty miles north. After this blows over, you're free to do as you will. For a time at least, I think you should accept our hospitality."

Littlefield tied the flap and they stepped from the wagon. The wind had a hard edge to it. Taylor turned his back to the storm.

"Accept your hospitality! Lord, sir, you've saved us, I reckon. Ran out of beans two days back, and been scavenging Indian potatoes and game since. Wife's about to deliver . . . I thank you. Thank you all," he said, shouting to the soldiers who sat their horses facing him, their shoulders and hats frosted with snow.

Corporal Miller touched his hat, Stretch Dobbs murmured something, and Phil Forrester bowed. Charlie Burns simply glared at Littlefield, spat, and turned his horse away.

Stretch Dobbs observed it and frowned. Littlefield, familiar with insult, shrugged. Taylor stalked after his soldier.

He caught Burns's horse by the bridle and held it with both hands. "What the hell's the matter with you, Burns?"

"Matter?" Burns, a stocky, ruddy-faced Virginian, leaned forward and explained with patience, "He's black as the ace of spades, Mr. Taylor."

"He's a citizen."

Burns shrugged. "That's Mr. Lincoln's mistake. Unless they passed a law that says I got to love 'em..."

"You will be civil to them, Private." Taylor was incensed.

"I'll be civil, sir. Keep 'em away from me and I'll be just as civil as you please. Can't help my feelings," he said almost apologetically, "and I don't reckon even the U.S. Army can make me change my heart."

Taylor and Burns locked eyes for a moment. The wind was hard against them. Burns's horse shifted its feet uncomfortably. "Sir?" Burns was looking at Taylor's hands.

He still held the bridle, and now, with a sigh, he dropped his hands, waving the soldier away impatiently. Taylor crossed to Littlefield, who had stood watching the exchange, his long-handled ox lash in his thick, dark hands.

"I apologize for my man," Taylor told him.

"For nothin'. A man gets set in his ways—we all do."

"I think we should travel on," Taylor said, looking to the skies. "Find some shelter and sit this out. It might blow over shortly. That is, if your wife can take the jolting."

"She's took it this far. When she can't take it no more, I guess she'll holler out." Littlefield smiled, but care was etched into his face. "Never seen nothin' like this weather. It snows from time to time in Alabama, but not like this. But you guess it might blow over soon?"

It was more of a hope than an educated guess, but Taylor told him, "It looks like it might. For now, let's find some shelter. There's a coulee a few miles north.

We can get under a bank on the lee side."

"Right, sir. Much appreciate it."

Taylor nodded. "Miller! We're heading back toward the coulee. We'll be out of the wind, at least. Go on ahead, pick a spot and start a fire. Break out some grub."

Miller saluted, gestured to Stretch Dobbs, and the two enlisted men rode out ahead. Cole Littlefield snapped his whip over the heads of his two weary oxen, and the two beasts strained at the heavy yoke, tugging the heavy Conestoga wagon into hesitant motion.

Taylor mounted and, siding Forrester and Burns, followed the Littlefield wagon northward, into the teeth of the howling storm.

It was a difficult three miles to the coulee. The wind, which had been unceasingly brisk, now roared out of the north, lifting the snow that had already fallen, hurling it into their faces. Taylor reversed his bandanna and pulled it over his face to combat some of the sting.

The canvas on the Littlefield wagon snapped and quivered. The oxen plodded wearily on into the heart of the storm. The coulee gaped suddenly before them, and Littlefield, braking his oxen, skillfully drove his wagon down the sandy, snow-heaped banks.

Through the screen of snow, Taylor could see a quick-running stream rushing through the coulee, twisting through the stands of gray, windblown willows. Peering northward, he finally picked up the feeble glimmering of a fire through the snow.

"Up ahead," Taylor shouted.

Littlefield, a scarf around his face, nodded. The wagon jounced over a hidden depression and rolled on across the stream, the snow nearly up to its axles.

Miller had found the ideal spot. Although the snow lay heavily all around them, drifted up against the windward bluff, a trick of the wind currents had swept the ground clean where Miller had located the camp. High-rising bluffs walled off the north wind and reflected the heat of Miller's wind-whipped fire.

Taylor had always been convinced that Corporal

Miller was sergeant material. He had demonstrated it again: he had coffee boiling already.

Taylor swung down and handed his reins to Private Forrester, who led the bay back against the bluff, where the other horses had been hobbled. Littlefield let his oxen stand yoked. The animals stood, heads bowed, rolling miserable eyes toward the men.

Littlefield helped his wife from the wagon gate, and then lifted his daughter up and over. The two women sat gratefully beside the fire, which flared up hotly, painting dancing shadows on the bluffs.

Clarissa Littlefield sat with a blanket around her shoulders, shivering. Her little girl, wide-eyed, peered out from the cocoon of the blanket. She carried a rag doll, and had her hair done up in a dozen braids tied with rags.

Stretch Dobbs carried a cup of coffee to Clarissa, who looked up, smiled shyly, and said, "Thank you. Thank you so much."

"Just drink it before it gets cold," Dobbs said. "That should take all of thirty seconds."

Clarissa smiled again and glanced around the campfire ring where Lieutenant Taylor, squatting on his heels, cradled his own coffee cup in both hands. Corporal Miller and Private Forrester were scrounging for wood among the willows, invisible behind the veil of the snowstorm.

Private Burns sat opposite Clarissa, simply looking at her until she had to turn her eyes away. Taylor glanced sharply at Burns, and the soldier shrugged, spitting into the fire.

"What is it with Burns?" Taylor asked Dobbs later.

Dobbs couldn't enlighten him much. "I don't know rightly, sir. He's from the South, of course. But I reckon there's something else that happened back in Virginia. Something that soured him." Stretch paused thoughtfully. "I do know he was Confederate. An officer, I do believe. And I know he lost some family and his property."

"How's his temper, Dobbs? I mean, can he hold himself in? If he can't, by God, I'll have him tied up until we reach the outpost."

"Oh, I don't think there's a problem like that, sir. I mean, he don't mean harm to nobody, he just can't abide being around... well, niggers, as he calls 'em."

"There had better not be a problem." Taylor was resolute. "This is my patrol, this is the army. Not old Virginny."

Forrester, who had proven to be a good hand with a pot and a fork, was boiling dinner. From the wide, watchful eyes of the Littlefield girl, it was obvious that she hadn't been eating regularly. Forrester glanced up, caught her look, and made a silly face, sending the child under the shelter of the blanket, where she hid, giggling.

Taylor smiled, but it was a smile that passed away with thought. Just what was Littlefield planning to do out here on the prairie?

He had his team of oxen and little else. Seed he had, but no iron plow. The land up here wasn't like Alabama, where a man could expect to plow with a homemade wooden plow, and could expect a long growing season.

Had the man any idea of how to build a soddy, or had he expected to find forests here? Without a house, they had no hope. They would have to survive a hard winter without food, virtually without shelter. Come spring, the long grass would grow, and with the spring grass for their horses, the raiding parties would come.

Taylor had seen many a dead man and woman on the plains. Scalped, starved, or dead of something that, in other circumstances, might only have been a painful inconvenience—a broken leg, perhaps.

He glanced at Clarissa Littlefield, who was humming softly, hands resting on her fecund abdomen, then he looked away, rising to stride to where Dobbs was seeing to the horses.

Dobbs looked up and bobbed his head in greeting. He was rubbing down his own horse with his saddle blanket. "Well?" Dobbs asked. "Is he a brave man or a fool?"

He was looking at Cole Littlefield. Obviously, Stretch Dobbs had been sharing some thoughts with his commanding officer. Taylor could only shake his head.

"Some of each, Dobbs. Like most of us, only some of each."

Malone was feeling close to ninety-nine percent foolish, and he was silently cursing himself. It was all the woman's doing, he supposed. At times they could cripple a man's thinking.

"We intend to take the mountain trail, Private Malone," Lady Hightower had told him. Her lips were set and her blue, blue eyes determined. The men, fools that they were, agreed insistently. "If we have to go without you as our guide, then so be it."

There was nothing else to do. He couldn't have cared less if the two men rode into the Medicine Bows and got themselves snowed in, but it was different with a woman.

He looked at her and studied the tilt of her aristocratic head, that fine, dark hair, the swell of her breasts, and he was a goner.

"I guess I've run out of arguments," Malone told them all. "You're a pack of damned fools." Chapel said nothing, and the earl snorted contemptuously. Malone looked at Lady Hightower again, nodded slowly, and said, "I'm worse of a fool. I *know* what I'm getting into, but I'll go with you."

Now they climbed higher up the eastern face of the Medicine Bow range. At nearly a thousand feet, it was already ten degrees colder than on the flats. The wind gusted fiercely and whistled down the long canyons.

Worse, cresting a small saddleback, Malone saw the wall of incredible blue-gray creeping toward them from off the northern plains. He knew it for what it was, muttered a slow curse, and told Chapel, "That's it. A blue norther, and coming at us like a cougar smelling meat."

"You mean it will snow." Chapel had a way of reducing everything to the commonplace.

"I mean it'll likely be a blizzard. If it hits us—"

*"If?* Then you aren't even sure of that, are you, Malone?"

"Sure enough to be scared."

"That I can believe," the naturalist said. If he had known Malone better, he wouldn't have made such a comment, but he was blithely ignorant of many things.

Malone tried valiantly to restrain himself.

"Well," Lady Hightower said brightly, "we've already begun. I don't suppose there's any sense in turning back."

"Turn back!" Whittington was incensed. "We knew it might snow. I can't see that anything has changed."

Malone muttered, "You damn sure *will* see it change, Mr. Third Earl, and change fast."

He looked again at Lady Hightower, but she was eager to be moving forward, up the winding trail. She was going on, no matter what, and Malone followed. He no longer felt a mere ninety-nine percent foolish. The wall of blue-black clouds advanced relentlessly, and the long prairie far below fell into shadow. Malone tugged his collar up and his hat down.

They rode a long rim trail along the eastern flank, and then entered a deep, shadowed canyon where walls of blue granite rose up two thousand feet or more to the rim above. There, cedar and wind-flagged spruce grew in profusion. Ice glazed the walls of the canyon, and a dazzling waterfall fell three hundred feet from the cliff face, into a deep basin, where it swirled and frothed, becoming a rushing white-water river that wound down the canyon, paralleling their trail.

Lady Hightower rode blissfully toward the uplands. Every way she turned she saw inspiration, a scene worthy of sketching. The cold seemed not to bother her, nor did the distant rumbling of thunder.

They lingered on the trail for three hours while Dr. Chapel clambered up a rocky bluff to examine a stunted cedar. He collected seeds and a section of bark while Malone sat his horse, his head bowed with exasperation.

As long as Chapel was gone, Lady Hightower figured she might as well sketch the waterfall and the corrugated bluffs of the canyon. She unpacked one of the horses, sat down on a canvas camp chair, and began to draw.

The skies darkened and Malone climbed out of the saddle, looking around with vast impatience for Chapel.

"I wouldn't worry about the weather," the earl said, tugging at his huge mustaches, his small eyes cheery. "We've all the equipment necessary to see us through."

"Have you?" Malone asked morosely. He half expected the earl to bound off into the mountains, looking for a trophy mountain goat.

The wind rattled down the long canyon now. Lady Hightower had difficulty keeping her paper tacked to the board. Malone glanced at her work. It seemed quite good, but he was in no mood to appreciate art.

It was dark enough to make it mandatory to find a night camp when Chapel finally returned, babbling happily about a subspecies of a subspecies, and Malone climbed stiffly into the saddle. He was no longer in a rush; there was really no point in hurrying now. With darkness, the first snow began to fall over the Medicine Bow Range.

They found a small, aspen-ringed park a quarter of a mile onward, and there they made their camp. Whittington had a huge tent, the bottom half of which was framed with hinged planking. It could all be folded up into a five-by-five pack, but, set up, the tent was a sizable square structure.

The big man was having a time with it, puffing and straining just to unload it from the packhorse. "You could at least help him," Lady Hightower said to Malone.

"I wouldn't be much help," Malone drawled. "Kind of tent I'm used to, you just crawl in and flop down."

Obviously, Whittington had expected Malone to do such chores. He glowered at him, unfolding and fussing with his elaborate tent, quite obviously unaccustomed to setting it up himself.

Malone unpacked the horses, wiped them down, and

picketed them where they could browse the scant grass among the aspen.

"Well, it appears you are more obstinate than lazy," Lady Hightower said, greeting him upon his return to the camp.

"Thank you, ma'am." Malone touched his hat brim. "A man always appreciates a compliment." Seriously, he added, "Those horses can't do for themselves. I figure a man should be able to, if he tackles country like this."

She stood, chagrined, as he touched his hat again and walked past her into the woods. He returned with an armful of kindling.

"Right here, Malone," Chapel said. The naturalist was also experiencing difficulties. They had an iron stove that could be broken down into eight separate, quite heavy iron plates. The problem was that it had to be bolted together to be useful, and just now, in the darkness, his fingers numbed by the cold, Chapel was having the devil's own time.

Malone ignored Chapel and walked to a small loop of the clearing that was better sheltered by the thick stand of young aspen. There he sat on a skinned pine log, stripped some of the inner bark free of his firewood for tinder, produced a waterproof box of matches, struck two, and, carefully shielding the flame with his hands, produced a roaring campfire that the wind bent away from him.

Malone looked across the camp to where the iron stove had just collapsed again with a clatter, then walked to his own pack, dug out a can of beans and some dried biscuits, and returned to the fire.

The snow was light, but it fell constantly, melting against the guttering red flames of his fire. It was incredibly dark outside of the ring of light cast by Malone's fire, and he did not see her until she was nearly at his side.

"May I sit here? Share your fire?" Lady Hightower asked.

She stood with her hands behind her back, dressed in a short sealskin jacket and an emerald green skirt and hat. The firelight caught the planes and angles of her face, intensifying her loveliness, glittering in her eyes.

"Sure."

She sat beside him on the log, smoothing her skirt. She held her hands out to the fire, watching as Malone scraped the last of his beans from a burned tin can.

"Didn't they get that fire started yet?" Malone asked.

"I don't think they've got the stove together yet," she replied. But she smiled, a soft smile that Malone had not seen before. She studied him musingly until his steady gaze caused her eyes to turn to the fire, to watch the writhing weave of the flames, the golden sparks that shot up from time to time to duel briefly with the falling snowflakes.

"I guess I'd better go over and get their fire going," Malone said after a time. She was looking at him intently again, and he asked her bluntly, "What are you looking at me like that for?"

"I was thinking that I should like to sketch you, Private Malone."

He laughed out loud. "You're joshing me! And hang me in some gallery?" That was the last place he had ever pictured himself being hung.

"You shouldn't laugh. You really do have an interesting face. Rugged, actually, especially your jaw line." She stretched out a hand, which reached for, but never quite touched his face. "Look at those hands —so strong and brown. Broken many times. Oh, Private Malone, you shouldn't fight so much."

"See all that, do you?" he asked, and the heat on his cheeks was not all caused by the fire.

"And more. Your eyes, for instance. You are a man who likes to laugh—yet I can't remember seeing you laugh at all. Not once."

"This trip hasn't been all that amusing, ma'am," he replied with candor.

35

"But you do have a sense of humor, however dry."

"Dry?" That was another word seldom applied to Malone. He smiled. "I guess so. Some folks do find me decent company."

"And the ladies find you amusing?"

"Amusing?" His forehead creased into furrows. "You could say that. I get along with women, of a certain type. Not your sort, ma'am. I guess you'd look down your nose at them. Like you look down at me," he added.

"Why, it's hardly that!" Lady Hightower said. "I assure you I am very democratic—for an Englishwoman." She touched her fingertips to her breast and leaned far forward, craning her neck to look into Malone's fire-bright eyes.

"Oh," Malone said cynically. "Now, that I understand. Of course it's all right. Impress me into service—God save the Queen!" He waved a hand.

"Mr. Malone." She turned toward him so that her knee brushed his. Her voice was extremely soft. "If I truly felt that way, I wouldn't have come to talk to you."

"I thought maybe it was just that you were cold," Malone said with a gruffness he didn't entirely feel.

"It's just that I've met so few men like you. Most of my male friends are educated and polished, so that there are few of the rough edges and spines."

"That's fine—I guess a man has a right to be . . . polished. They don't have a right to be stupid."

"They're hardly stupid!" she laughed.

"No?" Malone peered intently at her, his anger surging again. "They've no idea what they're doing in this country. And this country is like you say I am, ma'am—spiny, rugged, and right unfriendly. They'll get themselves killed; I'll bet on that. And if you're fool enough to follow along, you'll get killed as well."

"Why I'll admit they're a bit bull-headed—"

"Downright ignorant, ma'am. More ignorant than any Indian out here, more'n me. That's a plain fact." Malone was silent. He stared at the fire, feeling her knee move

36

away from his. When he glanced at her, her face was placid, thoughtful, her eyes downcast.

He threw a stick into the fire, raising sparks. Standing abruptly, he said with a heavy sigh, "Guess I'll go on over and start that fire for them."

Malone did walk that way, leaving Lady Hightower at his fire. The snow tumbled down from a black and rolling sky. There was six inches on the ground, in this sheltered location. Above the trees Malone could see a raging wind picking the light snow up from the dark peaks, spewing it out into the sky in long horses' tails. The aspens around the camp perimeter shivered in the wind, but it was nothing like it would be down the trail, Malone knew.

Dr. David Chapel and the Third Earl had finally gotten their stove together, it appeared, but were failing in any attempt to stoke a fire.

Malone walked to them, ignoring their glares, went down on a knee, and emptied the stove out.

"What are you doing?" Whittington demanded. He wore a bearskin coat and matching hat. He looked pale, weary. Malone ignored the question.

Carefully, he rebuilt the fire in the stove, opening the flue, which they seemed to have forgotten. Again, he used dry aspen bark for tinder. He didn't have quite the difficulty he had had with his own — it was far easier in that enclosed, wind-screened stove.

It took only one match, instead of two.

Secretly, it pleasured Malone that it had been so easy, but his expression gave nothing away. He stood facing them, let the wind snuff out the match, which glowed briefly in his hand, and then strode away.

That done, Malone retrieved his bedroll and returned to his separate fire. It burned low already, and he walked out into the perimeter again, searching for dead wood. He found a deal of it by feel; his feet crunched over small branches and he picked them up, cradling his armful of kindling. He was near to where the horses had been picketed, and he decided that he wanted his own bay nearer to his fire, and so he worked in that direction through the slender aspens and deep shadows.

He saw a shadowy figure suddenly, and he stopped, pressed against the trees. He doubted there were any hostiles around, but caution was deeply ingrained, and Malone held his position until he saw that it was only Chapel.

He started to turn and walk to his horse when he heard Chapel speak.

"Well, she got to him too."

"She could charm a cobra," Whittington answered with a guffaw. "Five minutes with Lady Hightower, and Malone comes hopping to light the fire." Whittington laughed again.

"She has a way with menials. Have you been to her manor? All efficiency. She has a way of pretending she's one of them."

It was freezing cold that night, but Malone's ears were burning and his neck was flushed hotly. So that was her only purpose in visiting him: to pacify one of the menials, to domesticate him.

He thought of the touch of her knee, of that soft smile. She was going to sketch him and hang him in a gallery! No wonder Whittington was laughing.

He was mad enough to spit, to lash out, but there was no point in it. Malone strode back to his camp, angrily throwing his wood down in a jumble.

Then he rolled up in his blanket near the low-burning fire, and watched the snow fall out of the dark skies for long hours.

# four _____

Morning was gray and windy in the high country, yet the snow had ceased. Malone ate alone, sullenly, without much appetite. When he was through, he saddled his horse and led it into the camp shared by the three Britons.

Whittington had apparently been elected chef, for the earl was stirring something in a pan on the iron stove, scowling and muttering to himself. He glanced up and saw Malone, and his scowl deepened.

Chapel and Lady Hightower rested in folding canvas chairs, behind a folding table that, incredibly, was spread with a linen cloth and set with silver.

"Good morning, Malone," Lady Hightower said with vivacity. She was smiling, and Malone read in the expression mingled mockery and amusement. He ignored her.

"Don't linger long," he said to Chapel. "We should be an hour on the trail already."

"Dear fellow," Chapel said, "what in God's name is your hurry? Afraid of your commanding officer, I take it. Don't worry, we'll make excuses for you; we do have some authority."

"That's not it."

"The weather?" Chapel looked skyward. "Certainly not the weather still? The snow has passed away."

"I don't reckon it's over," Malone said. "Even with what we got during the night, we will have a tough time of it in the high passes. Don't forget, we camped in a protected location. Up above, the snow will have drifted deep."

Chapel paid more attention to the plate that the Third Earl set before him than he did to Malone. With infuriating deliberateness, Chapel unfolded a spotless linen napkin, spread it on his lap, and poked at the unidentifiable, colorless food before him.

"See to the horses, will you, Malone?" he said. Then, to Lady Hightower: "He was merciless to the eel, wasn't he? Are these eggs?"

Malone spun and walked to the horses. He preferred their company.

It was another leisurely two hours before they had finished their meal, disassembled the stove, and taken down the tents.

Malone helped them with the tents and the packing only to hurry them along. Whittington had to take a rest every fifteen minutes, it seemed, and Lady Hightower prevailed upon them all to stop for a last spot of tea before the stove was taken down.

The trail widened and dropped into a high valley where scattered spruce, clad in new snow, decorated a grassless white expanse.

They had been on the trail only an hour, but Chapel, supported by the others, insisted on nooning there. It required unloading the iron stove again, laboriously building a fire, steeping tea, setting up the collapsible table.

Malone fumed; but his impatience was hardly enough to get them moving. After a two-hour lunch they started again. Now the trail climbed steeply upward, toward the aloof peaks above.

The river roared past, thousands of feet below. The wind was stiff, pressing them against the rising stone wall on one side of the trail, which, mile by mile, grew rougher, steeper, and narrower.

Lady Hightower began to show strain on her normally serene face. Her bustle rubbed the rock face behind her as she sat sidesaddle on her horse. Her feet hung over thousands of feet of sheer precipice.

Chapel was expressionless, but his jaw was tight with exertion and, perhaps, apprehension. Whittington was alternately crimson in the face and pallid as a ghost.

It began to snow again.

It came barreling down from out of the north, and it was no gentle snowfall, but heavy, wet walls of snow that filmed the rocks and trees in minutes, cutting off vision, darkening the already leaden skies.

It was as if a curtain had been drawn before them, and it came at the worst possible time. The path, already narrow, was no wider now than the length of a man's arm. The horses picked their way with the greatest caution and difficulty. One of the packhorses balked and refused to move.

Malone slipped from his bay and, squeezing between the horse's shoulder and the wall of icy stone, reached the pack animal. He used his coat for a blindfold and nodded to Whittington, who moved forward with the other horses. Malone followed, speaking soothingly to the horse as he led it slowly upwards, the snow washing over him, the wind chilling him to the bone.

Reaching a ten-foot-wide alcove carved into the bluffs, Malone told them how it was:

"We've got to overboard those damned packs." He was breathing hard. The wind sucked the breath from his lungs as he hollered at them.

"What?" Whittington leaned toward him, trying to hear.

"The packs!" Malone gestured with his palms. "We've got to dump them."

"Not very damned likely," the Third Earl snapped.

Lady Hightower, her face drawn now, stared at the men without understanding what they said.

"We need every item on those animals," Chapel yelled. The wind twisted his words. Beyond the alcove, the snow fell in sheets. The long canyon below them was completely obscured.

"It's your choice! The packs or the horses. They're too wide for the trail, too heavy."

Whittington took it personally. "You'd like to see that, wouldn't you? See our journey turned into disaster. All of David's specimens, Lady Hightower's work, my trophies."

"Damn your trophies! You'll die for a rack of antlers. I'm damned if I'll lead those animals along on foot."

"You don't have to! Who asked you to! The snow's bound to let up soon. I can't see the trail getting any worse, for God's sake."

"For your sake, then, I hope it don't." There was no point in arguing anymore. With each minute they tarried, the snow grew deeper. It could already have blocked the trail ahead of them, leaving them no way up and no way down.

Malone led out, Lady Hightower behind him. The lady didn't insist on stopping for tea this time. The trail, seldom more than three feet wide, was covered with a foot of snow; and now, as the stumbling, frantic action of his bay told Malone, there was ice beneath the snow.

He was grateful for the snow just then; he didn't want to look down at the bottom of the long canyon, thousands of feet below.

Malone halted and slid from his horse. He cupped his hands against the howling of the wind and shouted to the woman, "Lead your horse! There's ice underfoot."

She nodded with slow comprehension and managed to slide off her horse on the side next to the wall. Malone saw her head turn as she passed the word to the others.

Then he turned and walked ahead, moving slowly, the snow blasting his face.

He could barely see Lady Hightower, bent far forward into the wind. The others were lost in the blizzard. Malone hit a patch of ice and felt his boot go out from under him and slide over the edge.

He gripped the reins of his bay tightly, and managed to pull himself back onto the trail, gasping. The snow cleared briefly, and Malone saw Lady Hightower, her hands to her mouth, staring at him with unconcealed panic.

*The lady cares,* he told himself bitterly. Whipping his bandanna off, Malone tied his hat down with it. Chapel and Whittington had been forced to stop when Malone slipped, and now they stared at him in anger, probably suspecting, since they had not seen him slip, that he had stopped only to arrange his hat.

Malone turned and led the way upward. Briefly, through a ragged break in the clouds, he saw a high, jagged peak against a somber sky.

He glanced back at Lady Hightower, started to turn his head back, and then saw the frantic pawing of the packhorse. The animal had lost its footing on the ice, and the bulky pack it carried kept it from moving nearer to the wall. Now, in wide-eyed panic, it whinnied and danced an uncontrolled, wobbly jig. The panicked dance lasted only another moment. The hooves of the horse clattered against the stone and then struck nothing but air as it slid backward and over.

Malone had a glimpse of the horse as it began a long, slow cartwheel through the abyss below, and then the clouds shut out the vision, swallowing up the horse, which seemed to die at that moment and not seconds later, when it slammed, unseen, into the jagged rock of the canyon floor.

Malone shook his head and trudged on as the clouds folded around them once more and the snow fell with renewed vengeance.

What was it, he wondered, that had been lost, that

had caused the animal's death? An iron stove, a bundle of antlers, sketches of the sunny prairie, cedar seeds and mounted butterflies?

The clouds thickened abruptly and the day went nearly dark. Malone stopped. There was no going on, and he pressed himself against the wall of stone, feeling his heart race, the knife edge of the wind, the numbness that slowly crept into his hands and feet.

For hours they stood there. Malone had nearly decided to go on, whether he could see or not. Exposed on that ledge, they would freeze to death when night fell.

Finally the snow lightened, and the skies, heavy with dark clouds, were painted with the deep, deep orange of distant sunset.

"Let's try it," Malone called. "We can't stay here."

Chapel, no longer so self-assured, nodded. Behind him stood Whittington, looking like a mass of snow. His shoulders were white, as were his chest, back, and legs. His outsized mustaches were frozen, hung with miniature icicles, as were his eyebrows.

Lady Hightower looked ready to collapse. Malone led the way once more. They rounded an outside turn and found the trail flattening slightly. The snow fell only lightly and the wind had abated.

Ahead and slightly above them Malone spotted a stand of blue spruce in a sheltered valley. It wasn't much, but it promised relief from the wind—assuming they could get that far.

Rounding the next bend, they found the slide.

Snow and rock had avalanched off the slopes and blocked the trail for a distance of fifty feet or more. Malone cursed fluently and halted. Below, the canyon fell steeply away.

"We'll have to turn back," Chapel said, and there was a note of panic in his voice.

"How?" Malone asked.

"Just—" He broke off as it occurred to him that there was no way to turn a horse on that mountain trail.

"It'll likely be blocked behind us too," Malone pointed out. "No, it's ahead or nothing."

"Can you clear it off?" the Third Earl shouted hopefully. Malone didn't even answer.

It was fifty feet of snow and rock, earth and debris, piled in a wedge-shaped slide that tapered upward from the trail, leaving no visible horizontal surface as a foothold.

"Rig some packs," Malone said. "Essentials only. Then we'll try it."

"Leave the horses?" Lady Hightower cried, gripping his arm.

"Only those you can't carry." Malone said dryly.

"Good God, Malone!" Whittington protested, "I can't make it. Over that!"

"It's the only way, Mr. Third Earl. It's that or sit here and freeze. Or, if you like, start out along the backtrail on your own. But nightfall will catch you. It'll be a hell of a night—I wouldn't expect to see morning."

"No, no. Of course not." His face had collapsed into anguish. "Malone, I'm sorry— we didn't know."

A hundred replies occurred to Malone, but there was little point in heaping abuse on the Englishman. "Make up your packs."

"My God, my sketchbooks, my paints," Lady Hightower said. She looked around, completely at a loss. Malone shouldered past her and opened the packs. The first one he came to was full of elk antlers, mountain sheep horns, a buffalo head. He dumped all of it overboard, later unfastening the pack itself and sending it to the bottom of the canyon. He slipped the bridle from the horse; maybe the animal would find a way down, though it seemed most unlikely.

Methodically, he moved to the other horse, treating the contents—mostly Lady Hightower's belongings, her painting materials—overboard. The stove was on the pack's opposite side, and he let it clatter away into the canyon.

Setting the tins of food, the coffee pot, and other useful items aside, Malone stripped the second pack animal clean.

Squatting down in the merciless wind, he fashioned packs out of their blankets and the leather strips cut from the discarded bridles.

Reluctantly, he stripped his bedroll and saddlebags from his own bay, rubbing the animal's neck. "Sorry," he said under his breath.

That done, he fastened the pack to Lady Hightower's fear-stiffened shoulders, and a heavier pack to the backs of each of the two men. They accepted the burdens without protest. Their eyes shifted alternately to the heavy, threatening skies, the long gorge beneath them, and the mound of snow and rock ahead.

"God," Whittington groaned, "I'll never make it."

Malone said nothing; what guarantee was there that any of them would?

He took a deep, slow breath and eased out onto the slide. He sunk into loose snow almost immediately, and for a heart-stopping moment he thought the mass of snow and rock was going to slide away from under him, but it held.

Inching forward, he tried to locate solid footing and handholds beneath the snow. There were large boulders, not likely to slide away unless the entire section of trail went, and of course it was possible that this also might occur.

He was on hands and knees, creeping across the snow heap as carefully as a harem intruder in the night. Twice his foot started small slides behind him, but each time he was able to check himself.

Fifty feet—it was only fifty feet of snow and rock, but each second held the possibility of death, and never in Malone's life had time passed so slowly, had each inch achieved meant so much.

Finally he was across, and he stood trembling on the trail, his heart hammering against his ribs. He tried to make his voice cool, but his words emerged from his throat dry and throttled.

"Now you, Lady Hightower."

"For God's sake, no!" She turned her head away and buried her face in her hands.

"There's no time for female antics or highfalutin hysterics," Malone said cruelly. "You do it! You do it or die there!"

A glance at the frothing skies convinced Lady Hightower that this was exactly what was likely to happen. The storm was clearly gathering new force. Boiling clouds frothed over the mountain peaks. Not only that, but day was rapidly fading. There was only a band of red-orange against the dull western skyline to provide visibility.

She gathered her courage and inched forward.

"Use my tracks. That's it! Just follow my trail."

He watched as she crept apprehensively over the hump. Her face was nearly pressed against the steeply angled wall of snow; her eyes were wide with concentration. She was the one who would have the most difficulty making the crossing, but, Malone recognized, she had the best chance of any of them; the lightest of the group, she was not likely to cause a second slide if Malone hadn't.

She paused, frozen against the white snow, and looked behind her.

"Don't look back there!" Malone hollered. "Don't stop. Goddammit, keep moving!"

For a minute she seemed frozen by fear, but she began again, and in a short time she was beside Malone on the trail.

Shuddering, she fell into his arms, her body trembling uncontrollably. He held her tightly, caressing her until she recovered herself and stood back, patting absurdly at her hair. Her coat and dress were soaked through with snow, and fresh snow fell on her shoulders, yet she, through habit, tried to arrange her hair with nervous pats.

47

The two men stood there, stirring up their courage.

"Third Earl!" Malone called.

He looked bedraggled, battered, and beaten. With a resigned shrug he stepped forward, got heavily to his hands and knees, and crept out onto the slide.

The snow beneath him was colored a rusty orange, now, by the last glimmering of sunset. The wind toyed with the long hair of his bulky bearskin coat. He crept sideways, a stocky crab scrabbling over the jumble of debris and snow.

Once he looked up, relief on his broad face, and Malone nodded, smiling. The earl scuttled toward them. Reaching out, he used a protruding branch for a handhold. But he trusted it too much.

Malone yelled, and Whittington looked up quizzically and then felt the snow moving beneath him. The branch came free of the slide and there was nothing left to hold on to. Tons of snow broke free and swept him over the side.

Malone had a last glimpse of him—his face wore a nearly owlish expression, eyebrows raised, mouth crimped with surprise—and then he was gone, a vast wake of snow following him into the dark, cold abyss.

Lady Hightower spun and buried her face against Malone's shoulder. He stood without responding, his eyes on the depths of the gorge. A little snow still trickled over the lip of the trail.

"Chapel!" Malone waved. "Come on."

"A man's died, damn you!"

"Don't make it two. Come on, before it's dark."

"I'll end up down there as well!"

"Maybe. But it's a chance. You've got no other."

Chapel stood staring at Malone. It was obvious that somehow he blamed Malone for Whittington's fall. His teeth showed through lips drawn back by the involuntary tension of facial muscles.

Chapel closed his eyes tightly, steeling himself for a minute, and then he came on.

48

"Don't fall," Malone said, so quietly that even Lady Hightower, standing beside him, could not hear his words above the shriek of the wind. "Take it easy. Real slow."

Chapel could not hear him, but he moved as if he were following Malone's admonitions. Malone's tracks had disappeared with the snowfall, and Chapel made slow work of it, testing his weight each time he moved to a new foothold. Darkness had shuttered the skies now. The snow held a last, nearly luminescent glow for a few minutes. Against that glow they saw Chapel creeping toward them, his form a dark, crawling spider against the pale bulk of the slide.

And then he was there. Malone grabbed his hand, pulling him unsteadily to his feet. Lady Hightower threw her arms around him, and David Chapel stood there shivering.

He was not alone. Fear had knotted their muscles, and now, with release, they felt drained. The cold wind was gusting against them, its force increasing by the minute. It probed their clothing with icy fingers and found their flesh, chilling them to the bone.

"Let's get the hell off this trail," Malone said.

In the darkness and renewed fury of the snow, Malone was not even sure they could find the shelter of the woods he had seen from the trail. But find it they did, literally walking into it.

The wind groaned in the upper reaches of the trees, but the snow was cut by the ranks of spruce. The darkness was nearly total. Malone could see no more than a yard at any time as he worked deliberately and quickly to pitch his own small tent and, after several exasperating tries, to start a fire.

Lady Hightower was given the tent and heaped over with blankets. Malone and Chapel huddled near the fire, which did little to warm them unless they sat near enough to be burned. They sat back-to-back through the long night, blankets around their shoulders, the wind a constant howling around them.

The wind made speech impossible, and both men were too weary to care. It was for the best, Malone thought. He did not care to discuss their situation, which was desperate.

Trapped in a valley between ranks of high-rising peaks, afoot, with few supplies, they were quite simply snowed in. Winter had them in its grasp and had only to clutch them, to squeeze a little, and they would be dead, to spend eternity in that wooded valley.

Malone watched the snow fall, poked another log into the roaring fire, and slowly, prolifically cursed. He dared not sleep, and so he sat there, peering at the wind-maddened fire until his eyes filled with grotesque gold and red images. The snow fell through the trees and was swallowed up by the fire. It fell slowly, and slowly Malone's hat, his shoulders, his feet were covered with it and he sat there thinking dark thoughts of dying.

# *five*

Dutch Rothausen crouched beside the buffalo skinner inside the small lean-to that Cambridge and his partner had constructed of pine boughs.

The snow had ceased, but the wind raged. Picking up the fresh snow, it hurled it through the air, giving the impression of a storm. Deep drifts were forming on the windward side of obstructions. In some places on the backtrail, it was already piled six or seven feet high.

Dutch noticed all of this, but did not dwell on it. His attention was fixed on the red-haired kid who lay under a dirty gray blanket inside.

Harry Daley was scared and cold, and had a right to be. His eyes peered at Rothausen from out of a waxen face. His hair hung damply across his forehead, his teeth chattered badly.

Rothausen pulled back the filthy blanket and winced. The leg was shattered above the knee, broken in three places that Dutch could see. Blood smeared his mangled flesh and stuck to the dirty tourniquet the buffalo hunters had fixed around his upper thigh.

Cambridge looked expectantly at Dutch. Even this old, plains-wise hunter was a shade or two paler. Dutch shook his head imperceptibly. The kid's eyes were still on him.

"Are you a doctor?" Daley asked. His voice was constricted, much too high.

"Surgeon," Dutch answered. He could imagine how much he looked like a doctor. Dutch was a big-shouldered, big-bellied man with a florid face, scored with lines of ill temper. He was not known for tender feelings, but just now, studying the kid's face, he felt deep compassion.

Daley moaned and bit his lip as pain surged through him.

"Give him some whiskey," Rothausen said. "Plenty of it."

"It's all gone," Bob Evers said, looking guilty.

Dutch dipped into his sack, tossed Evers a bottle, and said, "Give him that. All of it, if he'll drink it."

Evers uncorked the bottle of brandy with his knife. Cradling Daley's head with his arm and speaking softly, he said, "Open up, kid. This'll kill it some."

"I don't want any more." Daley twisted his lips away. "Just do something! Shoot me!"

"Shut up!" Rothausen said. "Dammit, kid, just shut up. Drink that damned liquor. I'm gonna take care of this leg. You're not gonna die. You've got years of living ahead of you. But you got to cooperate."

Daley stared at Rothausen and finally nodded, accepting the brandy that Evers poured into his mouth a little at a time. Dutch rose, nodded to Cambridge, and went outside.

"Well?" the buffalo hunter asked.

"Well, I got to take it off. That tourniquet's been on too long, as you know."

"We had no choice. He was bleeding like a stuck

pig," Cambridge answered defensively.

"I know that. How about building a fire? I'll have to cauterize the arteries."

"All right."

Cambridge went off to bring in some wood. Dutch waited; he wanted the kid good and drunk before he appeared, meat saw in hand, wearing his butcher's apron.

Cambridge built a fire in a hollow that he dug out of the snow. The wind blew the buffalo man's hat away, but he didn't bother to chase after it. Stacks of frozen-stiff hides ringed the camp. Off a ways, two Indians sat in a hastily rigged shelter of their own, staring at the big man.

When the fire was burning well, Dutch placed the blade of one of his kitchen knives into the flames, resting the handle on a rock.

He followed Cambridge back into the lean-to, where Evers was working on the kid. Dutch saw Evers give the kid a drink that nearly gagged him.

"Yes," Evers said with a grin on his whiskered face, "and you could have been away out in Oregon with your momma, instead of playing tag with a big bad buffalo."

"I coulda been in Oregon," Daley agreed. His eyes were glassy, his voice slurred.

"But you wanted to play with the buffalo."

"I wanna play witha buffalo."

Evers slipped him another drink. Brandy trickled down from the corner of Daley's mouth.

"And up he jumped like a boogeyman. I warned ya, Harry. A dozen times, I warned ya."

"Ya warn me," Daley agreed. He clutched Evers's sleeve and the hunter gave him another drink. Daley closed his eyes. "Up he come a big ol' boogeybuff. Hooked my butt, I guess."

Evers laughed. "Yes, and you'll have a story to tell. Lucky the son of a bitch didn't eat ya!"

Tears coursed down Daley's cheeks. He laughed and cried alternately. His chest rose and fell convulsively.

"Lucky the sombitch didn' eat me!" he agreed.

"Ah, what the hell. We'll winter in Cheyenne in a hotel and see us some ladies. You like that, Harry boy?"

"La-lady. Some ho-tel." Harry Daley's eyes closed, then came open again, and he went rigid. He stared at the menacing bulk of Dutch Rothausen, clutching at Evers's arm.

"Who the hell is that!"

"Him?" Evers told the feverish kid, "New man, gonna take your place till you're well. Says he's big enough to knock them bulls down."

"Wish I'da been. New man." He took a drink. "Ain't good as me—ten buff an hour I can skin."

"He can't do but five, but he'll learn, like you did." Evers gave him another drink, but the kid never swallowed it. His head rolled to one side and the brandy dribbled out. Evers lifted an eyelid.

"He's out," the buffalo hunter announced.

Rothausen nodded. "Bring me in a hatful of snow, will you?"

Cambridge ducked out of the lean-to, and Dutch prepared the kid. Drawing the blanket down again, he surveyed the wound. When Cambridge returned in a minute, Rothausen told him:

"Pack that leg from the knee up. It'll numb it even more." Then he stood and tied his bloodstained butcher's apron on. Evers recoiled at the sight. When he withdrew his meat saw and knife from the sack, Evers had to turn his head.

Dutch got to work. It was messy, and he only got through it by pretending it was not a man at all whose shattered bones and torn muscle he worked on. He left the tourniquet on throughout the operation, until, at the proper point, he sent Cambridge to fetch the red-hot knife outside.

With it, Dutch seared the stump of the kid's leg. He sat back on his haunches, his own face smeared with perspiration.

54

"Well?"

Evers had a finger on the kid's pulse, and he shrugged. "I can feel it, but it ain't much."

Dutch put his utensils away, first wiping them with snow. Then he hovered over the kid, who was pale and as still as death.

"You done your best, and the neatest job I ever saw," Cambridge said, by way of consolation.

"Yeah. Don't count for much if he don't make it, does it?"

Cambridge said nothing. He was looking at the long, cylindrical bundle on the floor. "I guess somebody's got to do it," he said, picking up the blanket, which leaked blood as he walked out to bury Daley's leg.

With that out of the way, the three men brightened a little. They sat in the lean-to, drinking chicory coffee, checking Daley's pulse from time to time.

The kid writhed in his sleep, a sleep that must have been ridden by bloody, violent dreams.

"Well," Cambridge said finally, "he's young. He'll get that blood built back up in a day or so."

No one replied. If he made it, he would rebuild his blood. Then he could go on his merry way—an eighteen-year-old, one-legged kid in a land where only the fit survived.

Dutch rubbed his eyes, yawned, and sipped his bitter chicory. Without meaning to, he dozed off and didn't awaken until almost nightfall.

Cambridge was asleep in the corner, under a pile of buffalo robes. Evers sat at Harry Daley's head.

"He come to, and I gave him the rest of the brandy."

"How's his pulse?"

"Better, Sarge. I do b'lieve he's gonna make it." Evers smiled faintly, and Dutch answered it with his own smile.

Creeping toward Daley, he felt the kid's forehead, which was cool, and touched his thumb to the pulse of his throat.

"I can't do anything else," Dutch said.

"I know it. It looks like he's gonna pull through, though. Thanks to you."

"I gotta get goin'," Dutch grumbled. He never had known how to take a compliment graciously. It was becoming dark outside, and the snow was falling, although the moon showed clearly through a gap in the clouds.

"Maybe you should stay here," Evers said, looking past Dutch's shoulder at the snow, but Dutch shook his head.

"I'm needed back at the post. Captain'll wonder where I am."

Dutch shook hands awkwardly with the two buffalo hunters and trudged to where his horse stood, shifting its feet in the snow.

He saddled up and tied his sack to the cantle. Lifting a hand to the two buffalo hunters, Dutch turned his horse northward, toward Number Nine.

The moon was bright on the new snow behind him, but ahead it was a dark land. Shadows and snow blended together. All the familiar contours had been altered. Snow had drifted into hills and knolls, and Dutch had to detour constantly.

The snow grew deeper and the night grew colder. Reluctantly he stepped down from the saddle; the horse was having a rough time of it.

The moon was suddenly snuffed out by the banks of black clouds, and the wind, which had been constant, moderate, picked up again and the snow fell. It fell in waves, in walls, and Rothausen stumbled on. It was knee-deep where he walked now, and he could not even guess if he was on the trail. He didn't even know for sure that he was heading north.

The horse balked and then stood stock-still, and Rothausen hung against his saddle, peering through the cold screen of snow at the reluctant animal.

"Come along, Chief. It can't get no worse."

But worse it did get. The temperature plummeted to zero and below. The wind sledgehammered him. The snow was picked up and blown nearly horizontal by the ferocious wind.

Each step now was difficult. Dutch felt as if his feet were anvils. The snow was knee-deep and the cold air was like fragments of glass in his lungs. He clung to the saddle of his bewildered horse, fighting forward.

He wanted to stop, to rest, but that was suicide and he knew it. *All right, then,* he forced himself to think, *I can't go on.*

He was ten miles from the outpost and was not even sure any longer in which direction it lay. Nor could he return to the buffalo hunters' camp. He hadn't the strength for that, even if he knew which direction to take.

The tracks he left behind him were already filled in with drifting snow. He couldn't see much farther than his horse, which was at arm's length, and the angry wind buffeted him as he stood panting, shaking with the cold.

"I can't go on...can't go back." The horse rolled miserable eyes toward Dutch at the sound of his wind-muted voice. "Got to find us a place. Shelter. Anything."

The Bestwick boys had a soddy out here somewhere, but Dutch had never been there. And even if he had an idea where it was, he still did not know his position in relationship to it.

"Anything else? Any other shelter?" He looked around as he talked to himself. "Maybe. Over east."

Riding southward toward the buffalo hunters' camp, he had passed Settler's Bluffs. They were named for a man named Settler, not for anyone who had ever actually settled there.

"Along the bluffs there's some ravines." The horse shifted miserably. Dutch patted its neck. "Don't give up, Gluefoot. Along the bluffs...all right. East."

He had to move, make a decision, and so he made that one. He had to get off the flat plains, where the hard wind rolled over the prairie like a sea of wind and ice. Had to find some shelter.

So it would be the bluffs. They were to the east. Due

east. The wind had been constant out of the north all day long, and so Dutch turned so that the wind was on his left shoulder, hoping to God that it had not shifted.

It was a primitive compass, but it was all he had to guess by. He trudged on, keeping the wind on his cheek, practically dragging his horse after him through dunes of snow that the wind had rifted up across the prairie.

"Not so far, Admiral. We'll make it. You're a strong horse, ain't ya?" Dutch sank to his chest, struggled free, and stumbled on, his legs leaden, his face a mask of ice.

Not much farther, he had said, and he tried to make himself believe it. Actually, those bluffs were five miles due east through the heart of what had become a very nasty blizzard.

"About half a mile," he told the horse, which, even if it had had human understanding, could not have heard him from three feet away. The wind was awesome; snow curled past Dutch's shoulders like raging surf. He had no feeling at all in his body now, neither warmth nor cold, stiffness nor strength. His muscles moved out of habit alone, and he ambled on, weaving like a drunken sailor.

Once, he noticed with a rush of awareness that the wind was on his right cheek. "Couldn't of shifted that much. Couldn't of, Commander," he told the horse. He turned then and retraced his steps. "Only 'bout a half a mile," he said. "Might even happen on the Bestwicks' soddy. That would be snug. The boys call themselves trappers, but everyone knows what they hunt is loose horses—some not so loose."

Dutch slipped and went facedown into a drift. He lay there a moment. The snow felt incredibly warm, comforting. He closed his eyes and rested. "Just for a minute," he murmured, but the horse nuzzled him until he rose, and with shock he realized he had come close to lying down to die.

"Jesus, my brain's froze." He shook his head to clear it, staggering on. The world was black and pure white.

Nothing in between. Moments of empty blackness, followed by a flood of white. Dutch's legs were rubbery and cold now once again.

He stopped dead in his tracks. Just for a moment he had seen a light—a flash of yellow light.

Should he go that way? Was it a light? Dutch hesitated. The light was gone, vanished in the maelstrom of swirling snow, if light there had been.

"Come on, Scout," he muttered to the horse. "On ahead. On ahead. We could miss that light. We can't miss the damned bluffs. It's only a half-mile, more or less."

He walked on, fighting for vision, for each yard gained, for breath. Exhausted, he sagged to his knees, still holding the reins to the horse. He leaned his head against the horse's flank and, nearly sobbing, said:

"I was lying to you, horse. Damn me for a liar. I was trying to keep your hopes up. It ain't no half-mile to the bluffs. I don't know how far it is. Or if this is the way. Damn you!" he reared back and slammed his open hand against the startled horse's flank. "You animals is supposed to know the way to water, to shelter! You are stupid!" Dutch dragged himself to his feet. Clinging to the saddle horn, he repeated, "Stupid! You're stupid— I have to do the thinking for both of us!"

A tear ran out of his eye and froze against his cheek. Dutch touched it in amazement. "When's the last time— ah, shit! Come on, horse." He paused, gripping the horse's head. He put his face next to the horse's eyes and said, "I'm *sorry,* all right! You're not stupid. You know how it is."

He walked on, more slowly with each step. Here the snow drifted to his waist, and passage was nearly impossible. Dutch could feel his heart racing around inside his chest, a racehorse with red-hot shoes.

"Hey!" He halted, only now realizing why the snow was so deep. The drift ahead towered over his head, and he looked up, smiling faintly. The dark bulk of Settler's

Bluffs appeared momentarily against the white mass of the sky.

"That's why, horse. That's why—damned snow's drifting up against the bluffs. Come on!"

He moved parallel to the bluffs and finally saw an opening—the dark maw of a canyon—and he turned that way, towing the horse behind him.

Almost instantly, the wind force decreased. The snow was deep in the canyon, but without the wind it felt twenty degrees warmer. The bluffs stopped the wind, but there was nothing to stop the snow. Dutch walked a hundred yards into the canyon, pausing to peer right and left before he found a small feeder canyon that offered as much protection as he was likely to find.

"Come on. A little ways more."

The horse would not move, and Dutch turned to tug on the reins. "Horse? Please." Sluggishly, the horse followed and Dutch led it into the deep, craggy ravine.

"Home away from home, Ranger—that's the best of the lot, ain't it? 'Ranger.' I'll stick with that. Never had no name before, I'll bet. Army horses just get numbers— like me."

Panting, Dutch found a small cleft some fifteen feet up the sloping wall of the ravine. The horse barely fit in the cleft, which was what Dutch intended. He went in first and led the horse. Then, untying his blanket from his roll, he spread it over the opening of the cleft, anchoring it with rocks.

"Cozy, huh? It'll have to do. Honest to God, I couldn't of gone another ten feet, horse."

The horse blew and shivered, its hide wriggling over the hard muscle beneath its skin. Dutch slipped his saddle from the bay's back and rubbed the animal vigorously with his saddle blanket.

From his pack he took the ham sandwiches he had packed for himself. He stuffed them under his shirt to warm them and settled back, finding a position that was not too uncomfortable against the cold stone.

The smell of the horse was strong in this close confinement, but the body heat of the animal was worth it. "Just rest, Ranger. Just have you a rest. We're going to be holed up for a long, long while."

# *six* ─────────────────

Windy Mandalian bowed his head to the wind and moved forward across the barren patch of prairie. Here the snow had been swept clean by the swirling wind, leaving nothing but dark, frozen earth, although back a mile they had had to fight through four-foot drifts.

Windy held up, glancing over his shoulder toward Gus Olsen. He could see the dark figures of the other soldiers through the mist of light snow; Olsen had them spread out in a picket line, but wisely he had instructed them to remain in sight of the next man at all times.

Light though the snow was now, it had a habit of gathering its force and unloading on them at unexpected moments. During these periods, which could last from a few minutes to several hours, there was nothing to do but bunch up and wait for it to blow over.

"We don't cut their trail pretty soon," Gus Olsen said, speaking from behind his bandanna, "I'll be about ready to turn back. Maybe they knew this weather was building and held the cattle in Cheyenne."

"Could be. Could be the Indians got 'em. I don't know if we'd even find a trace of 'em in that case."

Reb McBride had drawn up beside them, his shoulders hunched against the cold.

"What's up?"

"Nothin'. You got any suggestions, we'll take them."

"My suggestion would be turn tail and get on home, but I don't expect you like that one."

"We'll keep on until nightfall. If the food runs out, I'm turning back. The agency won't like it, but it won't do any good to lose a patrol out here."

"I got to keep movin'," Windy said. The wind tugged at his long straggly gray hair, the fringes of his buckskin jacket. "Sittin' here jawin' makes me colder."

He kneed his appaloosa forward, and Olsen followed. The snow held back for another hour, although the wind was bad. An hour before dusk, it began to come down hard. Olsen was considering trying to find a camp when he saw Windy, fifty feet ahead, halt and wave him forward.

Riding at a gallop, Gus pulled up beside Mandalian— and he saw them.

The cattle, white with snow, lurching forward, were being driven steadily north by five cowboys. There were a sizable number of steers, but the five hands should have been able to handle them, trail-broken as they were.

But they were skittish, spooked by the weather and the ice underfoot. Even as Olsen watched, three steers broke the herd from one spot or the other, and an obviously weary puncher on an even more weary horse had to haze them back in.

"Put your chaps on, boys," Gus joked. Then he led them down toward the cattle.

They moved through the gloom of dusk and snow, joining the herd just as it was being circled up and bedded down. The cattle bawled and milled, not wanting to settle until they had grazed for the night, and there was no graze.

A tall man in a black slicker rode out to meet Olsen's party.

"Samuel Childes," the cowboy said by way of introduction. "What can I do for you?"

"Sergeant Gus Olsen, sir. This is Windy Mandalian. We're out of Outpost Nine, sent to help you to the agency, if help you need."

"Jesus God, I'll say we need it!" Childes said. "My boys haven't had an hour's sleep amongst 'em the last three days. Hate to admit it, but we're lost. Undermanned too, as you can see. Any of your boys here pushed cattle?" Childes asked, looking them over.

"All of them, except Mandalian and me. Chosen for the job."

"By God, we can use 'em. Welcome, boys. We got grub to offer, not much else. So if you like, light and eat." He looked. "Here comes Cooky."

Olsen glanced that way and saw the bulky outline of a chuckwagon approaching them through the snow.

"Much obliged," Gus said. "We've been eating light."

They rode toward the camp, which the cook had begun setting up as soon as he stopped his horses. Childes yelled to his men in passing.

"Keep 'em up! Keep 'em on their feet. They'll freeze to the ground if they lay down."

Olsen was no cowboy, had never been, but he had seen hundreds of buffalo frozen overnight and had heard tales of it happening to cattle in weather like this, entire herds frozen to death overnight.

It was a ticklish job, trying to keep the cattle up, but prevent them from moving. The cowboys, moving like weary scarecrows, flagged them with coils of rope, nudged them with the shoulders of their horses.

"We'll lend a hand as soon as we've had grub," Olsen promised.

"Cut yourselves out a horse from our remuda," Childes said, nodding toward the string of horses. "Yours look pretty wore down."

The cook had a fire going. It cut brilliant scarlet patterns against the gloom of dusk. McBride, Grayson, and Dockery took a plate of beans and ham hocks from the cook and squatted near the fire. After a time, one of the cowboys drifted in.

He was of middle height, square-jawed and bewhiskered. He joined them at the fire, his own plate steaming in the frigid air.

"Glad to see you all," he nodded. "I'm Jenkins. From down in Arkansas. Any of you all Arkansawyers?"

Olsen shook his head. "Not me—Wisconsin."

"Mebbe you seen weather like this, then. Whew, it's plain rotten! No Arkansawyers, eh?" he asked looking them over.

"Pennsylvania," Dockery spoke up. "Him too." He nodded at Grayson.

"Texas," Reb McBride said, without looking up from his plate.

"Texas? That ain't far from Arkansas, brother."

"To my part of Texas it is," Reb said.

"We got us another Texan. Camden Shoate, mebbe you run into him before."

McBride's fork had been halfway to his lips. Now he stopped and glanced up sharply. "Who did you say?" he asked, his voice brittle.

"Camden Shoate. Know the name?" Jenkins asked. He cocked his head at McBride.

"No," Reb said after a long pause. "Never heard of him."

Gus Olsen had been watching. He heard the tension in Reb's voice, saw the subtle alteration of the lines of his face. He watched McBride a moment longer, and then, chilled by the weather despite their proximity to the fire, he rose.

"Grayson, Dockery—how 'bout spelling a couple of those punchers as soon as you're done?"

"Sure thing, Sarge," Grayson answered. He glanced miserably at his plate. "Beans are damned near froze now, anyway."

66

He tapped Dockery on the shoulder, and the two men walked back to the chuckwagon, where they deposited their plates and cups before moving to the remuda behind the wagon.

Coffee was boiling, and Gus helped himself to a cup. He noticed that McBride hadn't finished his food, but he didn't attach any importance to it.

There was a single, weather-broken cottonwood where they had made camp, and it bowed and snapped in the wind. The snow drifted down steadily, and dusk and the clouds had darkened the skies almost completely.

Windy's and Reb's faces were burnished by the firelight. Olsen glanced up to see two shivering cowboys lead their ponies to the remuda, unsaddle, and move directly to the chuckwagon.

After filling their plates, they moved toward the fire, one tall and wide-shouldered, the other smaller, younger. Both wore shotgun chaps, which flapped against their legs as they walked.

"Howdy, boys," the tall man said, "grateful to see you. We—"

He stopped, his voice trailing away. He stood stock-still, balancing his plate on his palm. From across the fire, McBride was looking back at the cowboy, and before Olsen could react, Reb launched himself through the air, colliding with the cowboy.

They slammed to the snowy earth, McBride's arms pinwheeling. The cowboy fought back tooth and nail, but McBride had control, and he had landed two hard rights to the cowboy's jaw before Jenkins, Childes, and Olsen could tear them apart.

Gus pulled a panting McBride back, feeling the tension in Reb's shoulders. Jenkins and Childes each had one of the other man's arms.

Reb struggled, but now Windy had joined Olsen and they managed to keep the two apart. They glared at each other across the distance between them. Blood trickled down the cowboy's lean face, and he trembled with anger.

"What the hell is this about, Reb?" Gus demanded.

"Nothin'. It's just the way two Texans greet each other. Ain't that right, Shoate?"

The cowboy didn't answer. Childes glanced at Olsen, and there was concern on the trail boss's face. This kind of thing made a difficult job more difficult.

"I'm orderin' you, Reb," Gus said. "Let go of this, whatever it is. I don't order you much, but I'm doing it now, and you'd better heed it!"

Reb was still rigid in his grip. Finally, Gus felt him go slack.

"All right, Gus. I'm in control. Let me go."

Gus did so tentatively. Reb bent down and picked up his hat from near the fire. Shoate still glowered at him. His plate of beans lay scattered across the snow.

"I guess maybe I'll go relieve a cowboy," McBride said.

"I guess maybe you should," Gus agreed.

Then, without looking back, Reb tramped through the snow to the remuda; taking the first fresh pony he came to, a paint, he saddled, turned up his collar, and rode out through the deepening storm.

"Mind telling us what that was about, Shoate?" Childes asked his man.

"Nothin'. Man's crazy, that's all." He lowered a finger at Olsen. "Keep that son of a bitch off of me."

"Go get yourself another plate," Childes said, slapping his back. "Forget it. The sergeant will keep his man calmed down. You do your part, Camden."

"Yeah," Shoate muttered. He spun around, wiping his sleeve across his damaged mouth, and returned to the chuckwagon.

"Any idea what that was about?" Childes asked Gus.

"None, but I didn't like it. I think McBride has the idea now."

"Well," Childes said, rubbing his jaw, "I sure hope so." He looked to where Shoate stood, and then, nodding, the trail boss moved away himself, rubbing his shoulders to chase the cold away a little.

"You have any notion what that was?" Gus asked Windy.

"None a-tall." Windy shrugged. "And," the scout added, "I don't much *want* to know. I don't guess you want me tryin' to be a cowboy, do you, Gus?"

"No," Gus answered with a smile. "I guess not."

"Good. Then I'm turnin' in." He hefted his bedroll. "The cook's lettin' me hole up in the chuckwagon."

"Why, you old fox—you always get the gravy, don't you?"

"You got to be smartest firstest, Gus. I've been over the creek and up the mountain a time or two. A man's got to look out for himself."

Windy walked away through the falling snow, whistling dryly, and Gus was left at the fire. After a time, another cowboy, the one McBride had relieved, came in and they yarned for a bit about the weather, the Cheyenne, and cows.

Gus made his own bed under the chuckwagon. It was a miserable night, but he awoke to a brilliant dawning.

Clouds circled the horizon on all sides, but above them was a patch of blue sky. The glare off the snow was blinding as Olsen made his way to the morning fire.

Gus saw Childes cinching up his saddle, and he walked up to him. "Shouldn't have let me sleep," he told the trail boss.

"No," Childes answered, "I shouldn't have. But I owe you something for helpin'. Grab a bite. We'd best move 'em while the weather holds."

Childes swung into leather, and Gus walked to the tailgate of the chuckwagon. The cook nodded at a plate. "Saved you some, ain't too hot."

It was bacon and biscuits, and it wasn't hot, but that didn't bother Gus. Except for last night, he hadn't tasted hot food in three days.

McBride had his horse saddled when Olsen strode to where the remuda had been held. He took the reins and said, "Thank you, Corporal."

"Uh-oh. You're still mad."

"That's right."

"Real mad. When you call me 'corporal.'"

"Right again."

Gus swung his horse toward the herd. The two of them were lagging, but in a few minutes they drew up to ride drag. In the snow, it was no worse than any other position. There was no dust to eat.

"I couldn't help myself, Gus," McBride said. "Damn that son of a bitch—"

"Look, Corporal," Gus said, turning in his saddle, "I know what's up. You met someone from down your backtrail. You owe him something. Fine. You settle up however you want to, but not now. You get me? This is a patrol, *my* patrol. I want it right. I'm ordering you to stay away from Shoate, and if you're smart, you'll take that order as if it came from Captain Conway."

Reb was silent. He took a deep breath. He knew Gus was serious. There wasn't a man easier to get along with, usually, than Gus Olsen, but he was a no-nonsense soldier. He was right, they had a job to do; and if there was trouble, it reflected on Olsen.

"All right, Gus. You're right, I'll keep it under my hat."

"Fine." He came alert suddenly, his finger pointing to the right. "There goes one, cowboy!"

A yearling had broken from the herd and, bawling its head off, was running free across the snow. "Go get him, Reb," Olsen said with a smile.

"Yahoo! A cowboy once again!" Reb yelled, unlimbering his lariat. His bay was no cow pony, but Reb managed to work it through its paces enough to haze the cow back into the herd.

"That wasn't too bad, soldier." Jenkins waved and added, "By God, I've got a job for you down South."

Reb laughed and fell in beside Gus again, watching as the gap of clear blue overhead diminished and was swallowed up by black, ponderous clouds.

Within five minutes it had begun snowing again, but

with Windy riding point they were able to keep up a good pace, despite the lack of visibility. That man had spent a lifetime on these plains, and Gus swore he was on intimate terms with every rock and stump for a hundred miles around.

Yet by noon the snow was a wall of white, and the wind was a shrieking banshee out of the north. Gus couldn't even see McBride, ten feet away. The cattle were only an indistinct mass in the distance.

The herd had slowed, and now stopped altogether. Olsen circled to the point and found Windy and Childes in a discussion. They spoke by putting their lips an inch from the other man's ear and bellowing. Olsen got the word in the same way.

The cattle would perish out here, or be lost. Childes had already spent half his drive gathering up his herd after a blow. The men wouldn't fare much better.

Windy suggested holding them in Arapaho Canyon. It might delay them another two days, but at least they would arrive with the cattle. Otherside, both Windy and Childes doubted they would make it with a live herd.

Gus was nominally in charge, and it was his decision, but it was obvious that only one decision could be reached.

"Let's head 'em that way," Gus shouted. Childes nodded and called his flankers in to tell them they were going to heel over to the west.

They found Arapaho Canyon through a sea of whirling snow and a noon that was as dark as midnight. Pushing the cattle ahead of them, they moved as far as possible back into the canyon. It was wedge-shaped, narrowing and deepening as they traveled west.

They lost a horse, and very nearly lost a man, when a cowboy suddenly disappeared through the snow. The creek that wound through Arapaho Canyon was frozen over, and snow had settled on top of the ice.

The cowboy was there one minute, and the next he was gone. They pulled him, screaming and thrashing,

71

from the icy water, rushed him to the chuckwagon, and stripped him down. Gus and the cook rubbed him with dry blankets and filled him full of whiskey. The horse had frozen to death.

Camp was made beyond the dogleg of the canyon, where naked cottonwood and sycamore strained to stay upright against the wind. One huge, ancient sycamore had toppled over.

The cattle stood exhausted, hardly milling, barely able to hold their heads up.

"There's graze up yonder," Windy told Childes. "If we can clear enough of that snow away, maybe we can save some of these cows that are fixing to die for lack of grass."

With Gus Olsen, they had a look. Olsen vaguely recalled Arapaho Canyon, but had no memory of there being much grass there. Of course, he had never been this far in. Fortunately, Windy had.

Windy got down from his appy and, with his boot and then with his gloved hands, began clearing away the two feet of snow that lay on the ground in this semiprotected spot.

Brown, frozen grass lay beneath the snow, and Windy's pony moved forward to paw at it and lower its muzzle. Childes was dubious.

"It'll take a hell of a lot of work to clear this away. Likely it'll just get covered up again."

"If it's not worth it to you, forget it," Windy said flatly.

"It's worth it. I got no herd otherwise. I just said it was going to be a hell of a lot of work."

"It is that," Windy agreed dryly. "Have your boys break some long branches off that deadwood. Sweep across it like you would with a broom. Once the cattle see it, they'll dig for graze themselves."

Childes looked back toward the camp, where his weary men leaned against the chuckwagon, soaking up hot coffee as fast as the cook could boil it.

"This ain't exactly going to make me popular," Childes said with a sigh.

But his men knew the situation was tough, and though they grumbled out of habit, they got to it, Gus and his soldiers helping with the job.

Reb McBride cut a long branch from the sycamore and got to work with the rest of them. It was mad, in a way, sweeping away snow as more snow fell across their shoulders; but they were gaining some. Already a few cattle had wandered over, suspiciously trying the long-dead grass, which was cold and brittle.

It was not bad work once you got the rhythm of it, Reb thought. At least it kept a man warm. He worked methodically down a slight incline, swinging his branch in wide arcs. He was practically beside Shoate before he saw him.

"We got to talk, McBride," he heard a low voice say, and he turned his head slowly to see Camden Shoate leaning on a branch.

"I don't figure we got much to talk about," Reb answered. "Though we do have some business. We surely do have some business to see to, Shoate."

"You can't blame me—"

"I can't!" Reb exploded. "Who in hell else is there to blame, Shoate? You deserted. You got drunk on duty and took off."

Reb paused. At times he could still see it in his mind. He had been under Colonel Chandler, out of Fort Riley in Kansas, when it happened. The Kiowa were kicking up and they were on night patrol.

Shoate was standing sentry; that is, he was supposed to be standing sentry, but the Kiowa poured into camp, killing three men before the rest were alerted by the screams. There was a brief, bitter fight. Reb himself had taken an arrow in the chest.

Later they had looked for Shoate, figuring he had been

killed. But he had simply gotten drunk and wandered off. They found only an empty whiskey bottle and his horse's tracks.

"Three men, Shoate. Friends of mine. Paulsen, Jamison, Bird."

"Dammit, McBride! That was long ago, long ago!"

"No different than if they'd a been killed yesterday, Shoate. You're a deserter and no better than a murderer. I ought to leave you for the army firing squad, but I guess I'd rather do it myself."

Gus Olsen had looked up from his work, holding his back. Now he glanced to where McBride and Shoate stood nose to nose in close conversation.

"I'll see to you, Shoate."

McBride bent his head and got back to work. Olsen was frowning, and he watched silently until McBride was a good distance away from Shoate. Olsen was worried. He knew Reb McBride, knew him well, but this mood was a new one.

Whatever this was, Reb was dead serious about it—serious enough to ignore Olsen's order that he stay away from Shoate. He watched as McBride worked, his face intent, his motions overly energetic, nearly violent.

Olsen had never seen McBride like this, but he had seen it in other men. There was a fury inside the man, a rage building. It was bound to come to blood.

# *seven* ——————————

She emerged into the morning sunlight, blinking with the blindness of one awakened from a long, deep sleep, so deep that reality seems somehow weird, incomprehensible. Her hair hung in untamed profusion across her shoulders, and she wore a blanket around her shoulders, clutched at her pale throat.

Malone stood as she came out of the tent, struck by a beauty he had been aware of but not intent on. With her hair loose, she seemed somehow more vulnerable, more attractive.

Chapel walked to her and squeezed her shoulder. "Feeling all right?"

"Well enough." Her voice was soft and distant. In some confusion, she said, "I thought someone would wake me. I thought we would be traveling."

"The horses are gone," Chapel reminded her.

"That's right." She touched her forehead nervously, remembering it all clearly now. The horses, the Third Earl.

She looked up, surprise registering on her features as she saw Malone squatting on his heels, sipping thin, hot coffee.

The sunlight was brilliant on the snow and she squinted against it, walking to the fire, Chapel beside her.

"What do we do now, Private?" she asked.

Malone glanced up. "Just what we're doing. Sit and wait it out."

"That's ridiculous," Chapel said furiously. "Malone says this let-up means nothing. He thinks it will snow again."

"Maybe he's right," Lady Hightower said.

"Perhaps," Chapel admitted. "Either way, I think we ought to be moving. If it does start up again, at least we'll be nearer our goal."

"First off," Malone said, speaking to Chapel, but looking directly into Lady Hightower's eyes, "this storm ain't blown over yet."

"But we have *some* time, even if that's so!" Chapel objected.

"Time? To do what? To wander off somewhere? To try the mountain trail and get caught up there, exposed like that? That wind picks up strong enough to blow a man off that trail. There's no shelter at all."

"You don't know that!"

"I reckon not. But it's too much risk for me."

"We'll starve here."

"Not likely. It takes time to starve. But we've got a fairly sheltered position and firewood—as much help as a fire is."

Chapel and Lady Hightower looked at one another. She was obviously in confusion, he was just as obviously sure of what he wanted to do.

"I'm going out," Chapel said. "You'd better dress, Elizabeth."

"I'll be damned!" Malone came to his feet. "You do

whatever you damn well want, Chapel, but you'll not take her out there to die."

"I'll not leave her with you!"

"Think I'll eat her?" Malone asked with a drawl.

"Please!"

The two men had moved close together. Malone's smile was mocking. Chapel had his fists clenched tightly.

"Please don't," Lady Hightower said again. She held a closed hand against her temple. "Each of you do what you think is right. If anyone stays here, I'll remain until help comes. I don't think I can walk out, David."

"But this man—"

"It will be all right, David!" she said in a high, tense voice.

"I can't desert you, Elizabeth."

Malone spoke up again. "Just wait awhile, Chapel. Tomorrow, the next day may be all right. But if you walk out now, you won't make it. Let's all sit it out here."

"You know, Malone, I don't think you want to get out. This must beat your regular routine. A beautiful lady—"

"Freezing cold, hunger, hard weather. Friendly company," Malone interjected coldly. "Sure, it beats a warm bunk all to hell. I think the weather's getting to your brain, Chapel. The reason I'm not going to try to walk out of here is because it's likely to storm again, even worse. If it does, a man exposed is going to die."

Chapel shook his head and smiled as if he had a secret. Malone, seeing it, wondered if perhaps he hadn't hit on it accidentally. Maybe the man *wasn't* exactly in control. The strain on Lady Hightower's face was obvious. Everyone reacts differently to stress. Looking again at that smile, at the gleam in Chapel's eyes, Malone wasn't sure the man was tacked together properly, just now.

"I think we should stay," Malone repeated. "Sit this out, dig in."

"Lady Hightower?"

"I don't know, David. I just don't know." Anguished, she looked from one man to the other. "Do what you think is right. I'll be all right."

"So you won't come. Either of you!" Chapel was suddenly furious, and Malone frowned. The change was too rapid. The Englishman's emotions were running the gamut. He spun on his heel, picked up the pack he had already made ready, and turned to face them as he tied it on with the improvised straps.

"You'll be sorry," he warned them. "You'll never get out. Never."

Lady Hightower glanced worriedly at Malone. Malone started to move toward Chapel, but she placed a hand lightly on his forearm, restraining him.

"He can't get out of here," Malone said in a harsh whisper.

"You can't make him stay."

He looked into those blue, blue eyes, which searched his for a moment, and then he shrugged. "No. I guess I can't."

They stood together, watching as Chapel gave them a last arrogant glance and then turned, tramping through the ankle-deep snow beneath the trees, and out onto the long, barren stretch of the slopes beyond.

Already, Malone knew the man would never be back, and Lady Hightower, watching as the patch of clear sky overhead was overwhelmed by the surrounding darkness, seemed to know it as well.

In silence they drank coffee and ate the rest of the bacon that Malone had sliced into the frying pan. By the time they had finished their unsatisfying meal, the snow had begun to fall again.

Lady Hightower stood, arms folded beneath the blanket she wore around her shoulders, watching the tiny, receding figure of a man battling his way through the waist-deep snow. Then the clouds closed between them and the snow increased and she turned away, watching

78

as Malone stoked the fire, as the world went dark once more.

She came to him, swept the snow off the fallen log, and sat, watching the fire curl into the cold sky. Darkness rolled across the mountains, and the pine forest shook with the rush of the wind.

She said nothing as Malone sat beside her, hugging himself. But slowly her head tilted toward him and rested against his shoulder, and just as slowly his arm went around her, holding her as the storm raged on.

In the shelter of the coulee bank, the wind was lessened, but the cold was terrible. There were two fires burning in Taylor's camp, but the only way a man could get warm was to position himself between the fire and the bank, which acted as a crude reflector.

Cole Littlefield had drawn his wagon up as near to the bluff as possible. Inside his wagon it was warmer, and Clarissa Cole was heaped with blankets. Still, the discomfort on her dark face was obvious, and not all of it was from the cold.

"Gonna be along in a while," Cole said cheerfully. "Gonna be a baby with us in just a little while, Lieutenant."

Taylor, his hat tied down, his saddle blanket around his shoulders, nodded back, trying to smile. If Littlefield wasn't worried about it, maybe he shouldn't be, either, but he was.

The idea of being responsible for a newborn infant in this weather, under these conditions, worried him deeply. Yet he had never been around babies much, and Littlefield had. When he voiced his concern, Littlefield had answered with a smile.

"Ain't nothin' to worry about, Lieutenant." He shook his head and smiled, showing white, even teeth. "I birthed my older daughter and three younger brothers. Baby'll be borned, *whoop*"—he gestured with a sliding hand—"whipped under the blanket next to its mama's breast, and it'll lay there fed and warmed like none of us are, I'll guarantee it."

"I suppose you're right. It happens every day, doesn't it?"

"Every goin'-comin' day, sir," Littlefield laughed.

Still, there was an uneasiness that Taylor could not shake. He wished the storm would clear. He wished also that Private Burns would knock off the cold-eyed staring he engaged in whenever Littlefield or Clarissa was near.

There was no place to send the man. Of necessity, they huddled close together. Dobbs had sprained his ankle hunting firewood. It was all ice and snow only a few feet from the lee wall of the coulee. And so they sat together, Burns staring darkly at them.

Charlie Burns still refused to talk about it to Taylor, but Dobbs had slowly gotten the entire story.

"Charlottesville. That's where I'm from, Stretch. Charlottesville."

"I know it."

"We didn't have much. I lived with my pappy on a sidehill farm. You know. Times was rough, 'specially toward the end of the war. Pappy, he was too old to go; me, I was too young. He always said he hoped it would end before I grew another six inches, or they'd slap a rifle in my hands and take me for a soldier."

Burns was silent for a long while. Dobbs watched the fire, watched the snow drift past.

"Toward the end it got real bad. Charlottesville was burned. The smoke—you could see it for miles, Stretch. Folks was streaming out of town in wagons, afoot. We all knew the Yankees was comin'. I thought maybe we should go too.

"Pap, he said, 'What the hell else can they take from us, boy?' He was right. We'd had two mules, but the army took them. We didn't have nothin' but a tumbledown shanty and a hillside of rocks planted with kitchen vegetables.

"One day, Deke Rush came by. Breathin' hard. 'The

niggers've gone crazy,' he said. Seems all the slaves on the Brickford Plantation had been liberated by black Yankees. Someone got them all fired up and they was runnin' around burnin' and lootin'. Rush was scared, but Pap wasn't.

"Hell, we was poor, poorer than most of the slaves. Never held no slaves, never could afford them, never wanted them. Pap, he was uncommonly proud, believed in a man doin' his own labor.

"It was in the middle of the night when they came," Charlie Burns continued. "A snowy night, wind blowin' all around the mountain." He looked at the skies, remembering.

"They busted in and started throwin' Pap around, laughin' and screamin'—they had got whiskey somewheres. I grabbed up my squirrel gun, but this big nigger took it from me. He pushed me away, laughing, and said, 'You best get out of here, boy. Get the hell out of here!'

"And I did," Charlie admitted. "I ran and hid out in the trees. I stayed there all night, and just before morning I saw the smoke, the orange flames, heard the crackling, the pop of wood burning. They had fired the house.

"Pap was dead. Beside the shed, his head caved in. They had killed him and burned the house. For nothin'. We had nothin'!"

Stretch was silent. Burns's face was twisted with remembered rage. His chest rose and fell with emotion. Dobbs asked softly, "Are you telling me Littlefield was one of them?"

"Hell no, he wasn't one of them! How could he have been?"

"Then I can't see what it's got to do with him." Dobbs was intent, thoughtful. "Honest to God, Charlie, I can understand you being bitter, still feeling hurt, but man, it ain't right to blame Littlefield."

"They're all the same!" Burns shot back.

"They're not all the same, Charlie. No more'n all

Indians are the same. Some drunked-up men killed your daddy. Lord, I'm sorry about that, but you can't blame every man with dark skin you run across."

Charlie Burns didn't answer. His eyes glittered under his full, dark eyebrows. His lip was drawn between his teeth. He was seething, Stretch knew. He wondered if there wasn't something else to this, maybe a guilt Charlie had been carrying for a long time. He had run, run out on his father, although there had been nothing else he could do, really. Maybe, deep in his mind, he felt guilty for running, for being alive.

A scream of pain rang out, shattering Dobbs's thoughts. He came to his feet and ran toward the sound, his hand going automatically to his holster. Taylor was in front of him, and Corporal Miller had sprung up to join them.

They found Littlefield crouched behind his wagon, holding his hand, his face drawn with anguish. Taylor reached him first, and to the lieutenant, Littlefield said:

"It's broke. It's broke."

Broken it was, indeed. The fingers on Littlefield's hand were twisted unnaturally back. Already there was a deal of swelling.

"What happened?"

"Plain stupid. Plain ignorant," Cole Littlefield muttered, cradling his twisted hand. "The wheel, Lieutenant," he said, nodding at it. "Seemed like the chock block was sinking into the mud. I didn't want my wagon rolling off into the creek, so I made to firm it up a little. When I put my shoulder to the wheel, she rolled off the block nice and clean.

"It looked settled, so I let go of her so's I could block it. She rolled back, sir. Rolled back . . . plain ignorant of me," he said again, shaking his head heavily.

"Come on, we'd better see what we can do," Taylor said. Littlefield's wife was peering from the wagon, apprehensiveness evident on her face.

Littlefield waved his uninjured hand. "It's nothin',

Clarissa. Just a bump and a bruise."

Doubtfully, she nodded and withdrew into the wagon. As her head disappeared, the careless smile on Littlefield's face faded and was replaced by pain.

Private Forrester asked, "Want me to get Burns, sir?"

"Burns? What for?" Taylor asked with annoyance.

Corporal Miller told him, "I guess you wouldn't know, sir. Charlie Burns had three years in the medical corps."

"Medical corps? Yes, bring him over."

Forrester scooted away after Burns. Taylor helped Littlefield to a seat on one of the rocks they had rolled up beside the fire for that purpose.

Miller had collected snow in his hat, and they had Littlefield pack his hand in that to keep the swelling down and to numb it.

Forrester came back looking deflated. Taylor looked up sharply. "Where is he?"

"Sitting over there, sir."

"What did he *say*, Private?" Taylor asked hotly.

"I won't repeat what he said, sir. He won't come, though."

"By God, tell him it's an order!"

"Yes, sir."

"Mr. Taylor?" Corporal Miller spoke up. "I know Burns is being a pain in the ass, but can you order him to perform duties other than a soldier's? If you do, he'll simply refuse. Then we'll have us a court-martial situation. If he does give in and help Mr. Littlefield, it likely won't be with too kind a hand. If you would prefer, sir, I'll be happy to try and set the bones and splint it."

Taylor turned it over in his mind. Pride, anger, and will urged him to order Burns to do this job, but cool logic told him Miller was right. They probably wouldn't be doing Littlefield any favor.

"If you can handle it, Corporal Miller."

"I've done it a time or two," Miller said with relief. "Stretch, cut some finger-sized splints from the kindling, will you? Forrester, see if the lady's got any old petticoats, clean ones, for bandages."

He took Littlefield's hand from the hatful of snow and gingerly turned it over. "I don't think you'll have much trouble with this, Mr. Littlefield. It'll hurt like hell for a time, but if we set those fingers, it'll heal up—"

"Mr. Taylor! Miller! Mr. Taylor!"

It was Forrester, and they looked toward him. He had gone to the wagon to ask for bandages. Now he stood there in the falling snow, his eyes wide.

"What is it?" Taylor asked.

"The lady, sir." He gulped a swallow. "She's going to have that baby. Now."

"Oh, Jesus!" Taylor looked at Corporal Miller. "Can you handle that?" Littlefield obviously couldn't, not one-handed.

"No, sir." Miller's face was set. He frowned and added superfluously, "We never had no battlefield pregnancies."

"Shit," Taylor breathed. "Any of you! Stretch? Ever deliver a baby? A little sister or brother? Ever seen it done?"

"No, sir. They took measures to make sure we never did see such a thing."

Clarissa Littlefield yelled suddenly, and the sound chilled Taylor more deeply than the blizzard could. Cole Littlefield had started to rise, but stopped halfway. He looked with deep concern from one trooper to the next.

"None of you all? None of you has ever delivered a baby?" he asked in disbelief.

"No," Taylor breathed. "Unless—" he broke off and, clamping his jaw with determination, walked across the camp to where the lone figure sat hunched near the fire.

"Burns!"

Charlie Burns came to his feet as Taylor approached him. He had never seen Taylor so determined.

"If it's about that hand—"

"Shut up, Private! It's not about Littlefield's hand.

84

It's about his wife. She's starting into labor. Have you ever delivered a baby?"

"I have. Sixteen in one month, down in the Nation. Doctor was gone, I was left."

"You're the only one left now. You're elected."

"Her?" Burns shook his head. "Touch that—"

Clarissa cried out again and Burns glanced that way, his mouth drawn down into a deep frown. "I can't, Lieutenant."

"The hell you can't!" Taylor stepped so near to Burns that their noses nearly met. "Whatever the hell happened to make you feel the way you do, I'm certain of one thing. That baby who hasn't even been born had nothing to do with it. Nothing!"

Clarissa cried again, and Burns wiped his hand nervously across his jaw. "Are you orderin' me, Lieutenant?"

"I don't think you can order a man to be a man, Burns."

"Christ." Burns shook his head slowly. "And what if something goes wrong?"

"Did anything go wrong down in the Nation? Those sixteen times?"

"No, but dammit, I ain't a doctor!"

"You're the nearest we've got."

Clarissa moaned and then shrieked sharply, and Burns shook his head. "Shit," he muttered. Then he removed his greatcoat, practically tearing it off, and strode toward the fire, rolling up his sleeves, Taylor on his heels.

Littlefield watched him hopefully, and Burns said angrily, "I want some twine if you've got it, scissors, clean sheets—"

"Yes, sir. Yes, sir!" Littlefield, beaming, went with Burns to the wagon. Taylor halted, watching them go.

"Will it be all right, sir?" Miller asked.

Taylor had no answer for him.

He stood near the fire, accepting a cup of coffee from the corporal. The snow twisted down out of a blue-white sky, and Clarissa Littlefield murmured again.

Charlie Burns stepped up onto the tailgate of the Littlefield wagon, ducked under the canvas, and went into the cool darkness.

The woman looked at him warily. Her forehead was beaded with perspiration, despite the cold. Cole Littlefield sat beside his wife in a chair that had had the legs sawed off until they were only inches long. In the corner, like some frightened, small animal, the little girl sat.

"Better take her out," Charlie Burns grumbled. He nodded to the little girl, and Cole, getting heavily to his feet, his wife's hand slipping from his, gathered the girl up in one enormous arm.

"Mister," Littlefield began, "I know you—"

"Get on out so a man can get to work," Charlie snapped.

Littlefield looked at his woman. "It'll be all right, Clarissa. This man was a doctor's assistant."

She nodded weakly and attempted a smile. Then Littlefield turned and was gone, the little girl twisting her head, trying to look around her father's arm, not understanding any of this.

"How fast are the pains coming?" Charlie wanted to know.

"One after t'other, sir."

"All right. I'll get ready, then we can just sit and wait for a while."

Charlie used the crate in the corner as a table, placing his improvised supplies on it. He placed his clean sheet ready at hand, and then there was nothing to do but wait.

She moaned again, her head rolling from side to side, and Charlie winced. The canvas of the wagon roof snapped in the wind. The wind was raging. Inside, it was close, faintly musty.

"I b'lieve I might skip next year havin' a baby," Clarissa said, smiling at her own feeble joke. Charlie flashed an automatic smile and turned his head away. The idea of what he was about to do gave him the creeps. His flesh crawled when he thought of touching her. How in hell did he get boxed into this?

He looked at her again, watched her wide eyes, the paced breathing, the sweat that now trickled into her eyes.

Burns folded a cloth and went to her and mopped her brow, and she smiled.

Then he sagged into the cut-down chair beside her, watching as she went through the spasms of a contraction. Silently he counted as her facial muscles relaxed, as her body went limp. In twenty seconds there was another one, and a good one.

Suddenly, unexpectedly, her hand shot out and grasped at Charlie's hand. Automatically he jerked it away, recoiling at her touch.

He looked down at her. Her eyes were pathetic, hurt. Her mouth turned down with pain. Charlie closed his eyes and gradually shifted his hand back to where she could reach it.

He felt her skin touch his, felt her fingers go around his hand, felt a warm squeeze, and when he glanced at her, she was smiling, her eyes closed.

Taylor paced the ground near the fire, moving up and down impatiently, arms locked behind him. Littlefield sat near the fire, unmoving except for the moments when his eyes would lift expectantly and then slide away to the writhing flames once again.

Dobbs, who had cut a willow branch as a crutch after spraining his ankle, leaned against it near the bluffs, his face concerned. Once, his gaze met Taylor's and the lieutenant shook his head.

Then they heard it—piercing, unexpected—and Littlefield came to his feet, nearly stepping in the fire. Stretch straightened rigidly and Taylor spun around.

The baby's cry could be heard above the whine of the wind; insistent it was, plaintive. Littlefield rushed to the rear of the wagon, his face a mixture of deep emotions. Taylor was on his heels.

The two men reached the tailgate simultaneously, and then, looking at each other, they hesitated, hands stretched toward the canvas ties.

Littlefield took a breath and went ahead. Clarissa lay still in the corner, her face exhausted, joyous, limp. And in the far corner stood Charlie Burns. He looked around sheepishly. His eyes held what was nearly wonder. In his arms was a tiny bundle wrapped in a striped Indian blanket.

As Littlefield stood gawking, Charlie separated the blanket and a tiny clenched fist appeared, a small round face. Cole stepped nearer, his face glowing.

"A boy," Burns said. His voice was soft and he was smiling, almost, with embarrassment. He handed the bundle, reluctantly it seemed, to Cole Littlefield, who cooed and prodded at the baby.

Cole settled beside his wife, and she smiled. He bent forward and kissed her forehead, and as the baby began to fuss, he placed it under the blanket with her.

"Mr. Burns—" he began, but when he looked around, Charlie was gone. Taylor stood there watching, and he nodded his head outside.

"You rest, Clarissa. Rest and grow strong."

Cole rose and walked to the tailgate. Taylor followed him out.

Charlie Burns stood outside the camp, in the wind and falling snow. Littlefield started to walk that way, and Taylor fell in beside him.

"If you don't mind, sir." Littlefield said, and Taylor shrugged, watching as Cole went up to Burns, who still was dressed only in pants and shirt, his sleeves rolled up.

"Mr. Burns?"

Charlie turned around slowly, his face unreadable.

"Thank you, sir. You done a good job for us."

Burns shrugged. "It's nothin'," he mumbled, looking down at the ground.

88

"I wanted to ask you . . . Mr. Burns, I'd like to name the boy Charles."

Burns swiveled slowly toward Cole. The black man's face was diffident, hopeful. Burns's eyebrows lifted in puzzlement. Then he nodded.

"Fine. Fine!" Cole Littlefield was beaming. He let out a deep breath he had been holding. Then, unexpectedly, he thrust out his left hand, the uninjured one.

Burns glanced at it, and as slowly as he had taken Clarissa's hand, he now took Cole's. They stood that way, not pumping their arms, but simply clasping hands for a long minute.

Then Cole Littlefield turned and said, "I'd better see to Mama, to the little girl. She'll be wantin' to see the baby, I reckon. Thank you, Mr. Burns, thank you again."

Then Littlefield was gone and Charlie Burns stood there in the snow, the wind lifting his hair, tugging at his shirtsleeves. Slowly he turned his hand over, looking at it oddly. Then, with the barest fragment of a smile, he shook his head and walked back toward the fire. He was cold and there was coffee boiling.

# *eight* ─────────────────

Sergeant Ben Cohen came through the door with a blast of wind and a flurry of snow. By leaning his weight against the door, he was able to close and latch it.

Maggie was on her knees in the center of the floor, her red hair pinned up loosely, a brush and pail beside her.

"So now you've come," Maggie said teasingly. Her blue eyes sparkled. She rose, holding the small of her back, and went to her husband and threw her arms around him.

"What's happened?" Ben wanted to know.

Maggie was gazing up at him, holding him tightly, her ample breasts pressed against his chest.

"The usual—no, worse than usual. The stovepipe's melting the snow on the roof, and the water's leaking through the sod. I've done nothing but clean up and clean up again."

Cohen nodded. Glancing up, he noticed that the roof in his quarters was swayed nearly as badly as it was in the orderly room. The snow was heavy and getting heavier.

"Well, you won't be cleaning up for a time."

"No? Are you taking me to bed?" she asked mischievously.

"No, and there won't be any of that for a time, either," Ben said grumpily. "We're running out of wood. We're going to have to double up where possible. Pack some things; you're moving in with the Conways."

"*We* are moving in with the Conways," she answered.

"I'll be staying in the orderly room."

"Oh, Ben," she said with genuine disappointment. The years had not taken the edge off their marriage, and Maggie Cohen still hated being separated from her bear of a husband.

Cohen was concerned about the wood situation, more than he had admitted to Maggie. An expedition had been scheduled to go out foraging for wood the day after the blizzard hit. Obviously they couldn't travel in this weather, and there had been no choice but to cancel it.

The captain was worried, rightly, about the weight of the snow on the roofs. Wojensky was even now forming a work party to go up and try to shovel some of it off.

Saying goodbye to a reluctant Maggie, Ben Cohen returned to the orderly room. Snow was drifted up onto the boardwalk, and he had to fight his way through the wind.

The sutler was snowed in. A huge drift, eight feet or more in height, had been snubbed up against Pop Evans's front door, and although he had made an attempt to shovel a path, he had been forced to give that up. You couldn't run into Pop without hearing his complaints about the business he was losing.

Ben entered the orderly room, holding the door so

92

that it did not whip open. He dusted his clothes and then stood near the fire in the iron stove. His own wood box was nearly empty.

Cohen looked up as the door was shoved open. Lieutenant Matt Kincaid came in, rubbing his gloved hands together.

"The captain in?" he asked, nodding toward the door to the inner office.

"Home to dinner," Cohen replied.

"He's lucky," Kincaid said. "I just went by the enlisted mess to see what they're serving up in Dutch's absence. I can't even tell what it is. Stringy, sort of green." He made a disgusted face. "Where *is* Dutch, anyway?"

Cohen told him about it and added, "The captain's worried about it. Dutch is alone out there. And it wasn't military business, exactly. The captain more or less volunteered his services."

"Anybody heard from Taylor?"

Cohen shook his head. "Nothing yet. But he should be on his way back. Gus Olsen is out playing cowboy; they'll probably hole up too. And Malone never got back. Officially he's AWOL, I guess, but nobody expects a man to travel in this weather. Knowing Malone, he's holed up nice and snug at Fort Laramie, playing cards and testing the beer."

"If he's smart," Matt Kincaid said.

"Smart? I don't know if that's the word, but Malone's canny. Too canny to be out in this." Cohen asked, "Have you seen the list?"

"What list?"

"Over there. You and Lieutenant Fitzgerald, me, Wojensky and two enlisted men."

Kincaid looked at the list, which was tacked to the board on the east wall. "Sleep here?" he asked, looking around the already cramped orderly room. "All of us?"

"That's it, sir. The captain's concerned. If this weather

93

doesn't clear soon, we'll be tearing down the walls to burn for fuel."

"Damn. Well, that's it, I suppose. Fitz is OD. I guess it's up to me to move our gear over here. I'll bring along whatever wood's in our box."

There was a sudden rumbling sound overhead, and Lieutenant Kincaid looked up to see the planking of the roof buckling. "What in the hell is that!"

"Wojensky, sir. Trying to get some of the snow off. These flat roofs don't shed it too well."

Kincaid looked steadily at the roof. It was swayed now in three separate areas. As he watched, a chunk of soggy sod dropped to the floor, followed by a trickle of mud and snowmelt.

On the roof, Wojensky was trying to stand upright against the awesome thrust of the wind, and failing miserably.

The snow was piled three feet deep above the sod-and-plank roofs. More was falling, angling down through the cold, wind-laced skies.

He motioned with his finger to Holzer, who could not hear him—or understand him. Holzer had very little English. But the German nodded his comprehension and began shoveling on the western edge of the roof.

MacArthur and Trueblood bent their backs to it as well. Wojensky had his own shovel, and he began working along the inside line of the roof, staying a little back. That fifty-mile-an-hour wind had already toppled him once.

MacArthur discovered immediately that the snow was heavier than he thought. He was from the South, and hadn't had contact with snow. As he worked, the wind seemed to rush into his mouth and nostrils, sucking the breath from his lungs, filling him with icy needles.

It was desperately hard work under those conditions. His heart was working double time and the rest of his body at half speed.

He got a good shovelful, levered the handle with his

bent knee, and overboarded the snow. But the wind caught him as he tossed the snow and he nearly followed it.

Wojensky's hand caught at his sleeve and drew him back. He stood there shivering, nodding his head in thanks.

Wolfgang Holzer was going about his work methodically and cheerfully. It was unnerving at times; the German could accept the dirtiest jobs with good spirits. He did so now, one shovelful of snow following the next as he cleared his way back toward the center of the roof from the western edge of the roof.

The wind drifted snow over them, cutting out all hearing and most vision. The footing was spongy with some ice. Holzer continued to work his way toward the center of the building.

Suddenly his foot sank, and before he could react, his other foot followed and Holzer plunged through the rotten planking into the room below.

Matt Kincaid made a dash for the door, Sergeant Cohen pressed back against the wall. The creaking they had been hearing above had turned abruptly into a rumble and then a resounding crash.

Holzer came through the roof, snow and debris following him in a shower of destruction. Holzer landed on Cohen's desk and rolled aside as a big beam, made spongy by weather, overloaded with snow, splintered and caved in.

When the debris had settled, Cohen came slowly forward. He gave Holzer his hand and pulled the private to his feet.

Overhead, there was a gaping hole in the roof. Snow sifted down from the cold skies. Snow, splintered wood, and sod covered the interior of the orderly room, burying Sergeant Cohen's desk, blanketing the floor.

Holzer stood under the hole in the roof and glanced up, looked at Cohen, and shrugged. Wojensky's face appeared in a minute.

"You all right?" he asked, peering down.

Holzer grinned and waved, and Cohen, hands on hips, stared up at the corporal.

"I guess we should call off this detail now, huh, Sarge?"

"I think it might be advisable," Cohen said with a slow sigh.

Kincaid had just finished bringing in his own and Fitzgerald's gear. Now, dusting the snow off it, he gathered it up again.

"BOQ tonight, Ben?"

Cohen shifted his eyes to the first lieutenant. "BOQ."

Kincaid nodded and looked again to the yawning hole where Wojensky and two privates were still visible. Then, with a half salute, Kincaid tramped out.

Captain Conway came in five minutes later. He entered, frowned, and then slowly elevated his eyes. Cohen was trying to organize his papers in a wooden box, prior to moving temporarily out.

To Conway's questioning glance, Cohen said, "Holzer. He's all right. I called off the detail."

Captain Conway merely nodded. Entering his office, he collected a few papers, which he tucked under his coat. "Headquarters is over home for the time being, Sergeant."

"Yes, sir."

Conway supposed there was some humor in this, but he could not see it just then. He walked through the heavy weather toward his quarters, wondering what could go wrong next.

There was a real danger of freezing if they didn't find a wood supply soon. Doubling up on the living quarters would help, but it was only a stopgap measure. On top of that, he had eleven officers and men, plus one civilian scout, out in that blizzard somewhere. Or perhaps he shouldn't count Malone.

Malone was an old hand and wouldn't be extending himself for the army's sake. He was undoubtedly holed up at Fort Laramie.

Of them all, it was Dutch he worried about.

He told Flora why. "He's alone and wasn't carrying any food to speak of. Probably no matches. Dutch is a good cook, but a plainsman?"

"Don't worry, dear, I'm sure he probably decided to shelter up with the buffalo hunters. They would have food and a fire."

"I don't know." Flora sat on his lap and he hugged her, kissing her shoulder lightly. "Dutch would want to get back here, knowing Farnsworth is—"

"Incapable?" Flora prompted, toying with his hair.

"Well, nearly so. At least in Dutch's eyes. And I've known Rothausen long enough to know that he just plain doesn't care for most people enough to want to stay around them. No, I think he would try to make it back, and if so, he should have been here."

"You're blaming yourself," Flora said softly. "How can you, Warner? A man was injured. To save a life, you sent Dutch. You can't be blamed for the weather, dear."

"No, I suppose not," he answered, but that wasn't the way he felt inside. He leaned back in the chair, feeling the press of Flora's breasts against him. She smiled and her lips met his. They were soft, supple, and she teased his mouth.

Warner felt himself relaxing, and put his arms around Flora, kissing her in return.

It was then that the door was rapped on, and Conway scowled and shrugged. Cohen was there, carrying a box of official papers.

"I think this is all we'll need, sir. I put some documents into the safe—they'll be secure there. Hello, Flora." Cohen paused suddenly. He looked at his commanding officer's face and then at Mrs. Conway's face. He sensed something then, an awkward displeasure, and he knew.

"I'm sorry, sir, if . . . you did say headquarters would be set up here, didn't you?" Cohen felt the fool.

"Yes. Of course, Sergeant. Flora, will you see if

we've any coffee left?"

"Yes, of course." She looked then at Ben Cohen, and her smile was warm, but she said in a low voice, "Nice timing, Sergeant."

"Yes, ma'am," Cohen replied automatically. Then, amazingly, he flushed slightly and got into his work. "Regiment will want a report of storm damage, sir. I found a file copy of last year's winter report..."

Captain Conway was hardly listening. Outside, the snow fell. Through the frost-glazed window he could dimly see the heavy drifting, the waves of wind-driven snow.

Flora was right, of course. He wasn't responsible for the weather. But he was responsible for the men he had sent out into it. And with each passing hour, the possibility grew stronger that some of them might not be making it back.

Flora handed him his coffee and he sat down to work, listening to the wind shrieking in the eaves and half listening for a cry from the gate guards, telling him that someone was coming in.

# nine _____

Breathing roughly, Malone stepped back to admire his work. The altitude had gotten to him more than he had expected. Each breath seemed to wrinkle up his lungs and expand them to their limits. When he exhaled, it was like emptying a dry, brittle bellows. But he had gotten the job done.

He examined it carefully. Was there a refinement he could make? Something forgotten? He could think of nothing.

He had taken new snow and piled it six feet high around the tent and some eight feet from it, forming a ring. He had then packed it down with feet and hands, glazing it. Malone now had an ice wall that cut the wind and reflected the warmth of his fire effectively.

With pine boughs cut from the forest, he had built a lean-to over the tent, and walls beside it for further protection. The snow, which had held back for an hour, now fell again, but Malone was nearly warm inside the circle of ice.

While in the woods, he had set half a dozen snares along the game trails he had observed in the snow, and taken the time to drag in dead wood. He had no idea how long the blizzard would last, and he wanted to be ready. They would survive.

She sat near the fire, watching him in the gray light. She looked weary, her hair down across her narrow shoulders, her blanket frosted with snow, her eyes large and distant.

"Better?" he asked with a smile. Lady Hightower nodded weakly.

The trees beyond the camp swayed in concert, moving at the whim of the wind, but here there was only a slight, swirling breeze. The walls of ice winked with firelight, reflecting the heat, illuminating this small eye of warmth and shelter in the heart of a gray mountain wilderness.

Malone went to the pot and tried his own cooking — Indian potatoes dug from beneath the snow, shaved jerky, and tinned corn saved from the lady's supply pack.

He grunted. The food was at least palatable, and it was hot; he had burned the tip of his tongue. He swiveled toward Lady Hightower, still crouched down, and told her:

"It's warm, and I reckon it won't kill you."

"I can't eat."

"I would, if I were you. I'll just have to save it, and it won't make much of a breakfast."

"All right. A little."

Malone nodded. Darkness was coming, and the firelight, dancing around them in a glassy circle, seemed eerie, haunting. He spooned a little of his rough stew onto a tin plate, filled a plate for himself, and walked to where she sat on the peeled log.

"Sorry the china's all gone," he said, handing her the tin plate.

"That's not a very nice reminder."

"Sorry. I didn't mean anything by it."

She nodded her forgiveness and ate slowly, picking

100

at the bland dinner. Malone watched her, watched the glimmer of firelight on her pale cheeks, in her eyes. The edge of her small, pink ear was visible behind the veil of her dark hair.

Then he ate his own food, rapidly, washing it down with melted snow.

"The same thing for breakfast?" she asked.

He turned to her in the near darkness, trying to make his voice confident, to offset the grim fear she felt.

"No. I've set some snares. We'll have rabbit, likely. There's plenty out there—snowshoes. It'll be tasty. Not the best food. There's no fat on a rabbit, and in this kind of weather you need fat meat. People have been known to starve to death on a diet of rabbit meat—" Hastily he added, "Of course, that was over a long winter."

"Yes."

Her eyes were downcast, her voice melancholy. Her wide mouth turned down heavily, and Malone kicked himself mentally for being such a fool.

He took her plate from her limp hand and set about scrubbing both of their plates clean with snow. Done, he squatted by the glow of the fire, watching the coffee boil.

He was aware of Lady Hightower at his shoulder, and he glanced up to see her standing there, watching him with a soft, indefinable expression.

"It'll be all right," he said with a smile.

"Yes." But she thought of David Chapel and Charles Whittington, and she knew that things would never be quite right again in her life.

She was cold, although nowhere near as cold as she had been before Malone had built this shelter. She was hungry, and afraid. Afraid of dying out here.

She envied Malone, wondered where he got his strength. She felt a sudden flush of relief; if she had elected to go with David instead of staying here . . .

She watched Malone work, building up the fire. She studied his rugged face, the whisker-blurred line of his

101

jaw. If only he weren't a . . . *private*.

Yet he was all she had; her life, she realized, depended on him. He would provide for her, keep her warm, fill her stomach. And when it was possible, he would lead her out of these damnable mountains.

Darkness had fallen and the icy wind had picked up once more, fanning the flames. All was darkness outside of the ring of ice illuminated by the fire. Lady Hightower felt suddenly weary. She wanted to sleep, to make time pass in that way.

She rose. "I'm turning in now, Private Malone."

"All right." Malone nodded, returning his attention to the fire.

"Good night."

"Night, ma'am."

She hesitated and then went to the shelter. The lean-to built around the tent had been so carefully constructed, with each branch overlapping the next, that not a whisper of wind ruffled the canvas of the tent.

Malone had made a mat of boughs beneath the tent floor to insulate and cushion it. He had made another mattress of pine boughs beneath the blankets Lady Hightower slept on.

She undressed, her teeth chattering. Once inside her bed, however, she was as warm and snug as she would have been in her own manor in Lancashire. Warmer, as far as that went. There was no heating the old stone house in winter.

She closed her eyes, not sleeping, but drifting through a swirling, colorless web of tangled thoughts. The sound of three rapid shots shattered that web and she sat bolt upright, her heart pounding.

She went to the entrance of the tent and looked out with trepidation. Malone was there, crouched over something gray and indistinct.

He turned around, his rifle in his hand, and she saw what he had shot. A tiny gasp escaped her lips and she clutched her thin nightdress together.

"A wolf!"

"Sorry to wake you, ma'am." Malone stood. "He's all gaunted up, half crazy with hunger, I guess, to come around this fire and man-scent."

"Are there others?" she asked, forgetting herself, coming out into the firelight wearing only her thin nightdress. The flames, reflected all around her by the ice wall, made her gown transparent, and Malone's eyes swept over her, taking in the swell of her hips, the thrust of her full breasts, the dark, taut nipples, the patch of darkness between her tapered thighs.

"I doubt there'll be any others, Lady Hightower. Just this old lonesome lobo."

"But you can't be sure?"

"No. No way of being sure."

Shuddering, she ducked into the tent, a ghastly memory returning to her. Her Russian cousin and her cousin's fiance had been attacked by wolves. Attacked and killed. She had been young when that had happened, but the event had provided her with many sleepless nights as a girl.

Now she crawled into the bed, her eyes searching the dark corners of the tent. "You're being foolish," she told herself. It was the weariness, the tenseness of the situation. Malone was out there. If there were any other wolves, he would kill them too.

Malone was there.

She closed her eyes and sleep, amazingly, came quickly. It was a deep sleep. A hiding away. Her mind refused to think, to dream, to retain alertness. She was lost in empty blackness until just before midnight.

She heard the wolves howling, and one lunged at her throat, its yellow eyes glittering, its slavering jaws open to reveal long, yellow-white teeth. She screamed and fought back. Screamed again.

She sat up, her heart pounding. It was dark and still, and the dream had gone, leaving her pulse racing, her skin crawling.

She heard footsteps and looked to the tent flap.

"You all right?" Malone asked.

He stood there, rifle in hand, backlighted by the fire, holding a blanket around his shoulders. The wind shifted the fire and his shadow danced around the interior of the tent, searching every corner.

"Come in, Malone," she said. "Please come in."

"Ma'am?" He ducked into the tent and stood there, his hat frosted with snow, his eyes concerned, shadowed under his brow. "Are you all right?"

"It was nothing. I was afraid." She looked at him, and suddenly lifted trembling arms to him. "Come in, please. I'm frightened. I'm alone. Malone . . ."

He came forward, and the tent flap, closing behind him, shut out the firelight. She felt him moving closer to her bed. Reaching out, she found his hand and he sank beside her.

Tentatively he bent his head to hers and kissed her. It was a long, searching kiss. Her lips were fluid, warm, and she drew back the blankets.

Malone undressed and slipped in beside her, holding her for a moment, feeling her warmth, the contours of her body against his, the rise and fall of her breast. He wondered if he was dreaming. Could this be happening?

Her hands clutched his shoulders, ran down the knuckles of his spine, found his hips, and she drew him to her. Malone followed willingly.

Her throat pulsed beneath his lips. His whiskers scratched her flesh, but she did not withdraw. She held him closer, guiding his mouth to her breasts, and he snuggled between them, administering tiny kisses along the curvature of her cleavage, finding her nipples, sucking quietly as she stroked his head, his bare back.

She shifted and Malone drew back, but she only wanted to draw her nightdress up over her hips. Taking Malone's rough hand in her own, she guided it between her thighs. His fingers crept through the soft, downy patch of hair and touched her smooth warmth.

Lady Hightower let her head loll back. She closed her

eyes in feline comfort, feeling him toy with her, spread her, probe her. She spread her thighs lazily and felt Malone shift, felt him crawl between her legs and position himself.

She felt his chest against her breasts, his hard thighs against hers, felt the head of his erection touch her and then enter her sharply.

He was far from gentle, far from deft, but it didn't matter. He plunged into her, pummeling her into forgetfulness.

Malone was deep within her. She was warm and the night was cold. She was soft and yielding beneath him. Her thighs wrapped around his, and her throat murmured tiny sounds. He gripped her buttocks and drove himself into her, wanting to split her, to dive inside of that warmth.

She answered his urgent thrusting with her own swaying, gently rolling motion. Her head stretched out toward his, and he met her lips with a hard kiss. He drummed against her, liking the slick, swelling motion of her, the fluid rise and fall of her hips.

It was maddening, demanding. Her breasts were bare to his kisses, her mouth was open to his—sweet and eager. He plunged into her again and again, his abdomen taut, his face set tightly. Her fingers dropped between his legs and he felt them toy with the emerging inches of his shaft, then crawl along to cup his taut scrotum, pulling him deeper yet.

Her legs lifted higher, rolling her knees away from him, lifting her buttocks high into the air, and by the faint gleam of the firelight that leaked into the dark tent, he could see her eyes, half closed, her slack mouth, the small beads of perspiration on her upper lip. All of it excited him, urged him on.

He was aware of it all at once. The scent of her, the clasp of her thighs, silky and strong, the sensuality of her face, and he felt his orgasm rising, felt his thighs trembling.

105

He locked his legs and lifted himself above her, driving his pelvis against hers as she caressed his inner thighs, ran her fingers up toward the tail of his spine, spread herself still wider, the frantic clutching of her hands urging him on.

She suddenly began to writhe against him. To claw at him in what was nearly desperation. Her breathing was throttled, quick, and Malone could no longer hold back.

He drove against her, filling her with his excitement, and she laughed once, out loud, as he came with a rush, sagging against her where he lay, continuing his motions on a smaller scale, his body pressed against the length of hers, her lips searching his whiskered face, his mouth, touching the lobes of his ears, her softly murmured words of pleasure indistinct.

Elizabeth Hightower relaxed then, completely. Every nerve in her body tingled, every muscle felt suddenly flaccid, numb.

He lay on top of her, his scent earthy, musky. Her fingers ran along the cords of shoulder muscle, down his strong back. Still he pulsed inside of her, and that was pleasantly reassuring.

He was a savage lover, a needing man. Yet he was strong and kind. He seemed to be asleep now. His breath fluttered and his chest rose and fell evenly. It was uncomfortable having him there on top of her, and her own breathing was difficult. But he was there. Strong and reassuring. The wolves would not dare come again that night.

The air was musty, stale, the scent nearly overpowering in its muskiness. Somehow he had fallen asleep, and now he came around to find himself nearly suffocating.

Dutch tried to move, and found his horse's leg pressed against him. Gently he prodded the leg aside, and the tail of the horse switched, slapping him in the face.

He stood with a sudden rush of awareness. He was beneath his blanket, trapped in a wedge of rock, with only his horse for company and, indeed, only the animal's body heat for warmth.

Dutch straightened up, reaching for the corner of the blanket. No matter how cold it was outside, he wanted some of that fresh air.

He grasped the corner of the blanket and tugged. Immediately an avalanche of snow fell into the alcove, smashing into his face. Dutch looked away, wiping his face. Then, slowly, he opened the blanket again.

His throat constricted. There was no sky to be seen. Nothing but snow. It had piled over him as he slept, and he felt a moment of panic.

It was bitingly cold, but at the moment that did not concern him. He was suddenly deathly afraid of suffocating to death.

Desperately he pawed at the snow, crumbling it down upon him again. It was a delicate situation. He knew that if he was careless, the mass of snow could break free. Falling into the crevice, it would smother both him and the horse to death.

Looking around in the musty darkness, Dutch picked up his rifle. Jabbing cautiously at the snow, he thrust the barrel of the Springfield into the snow.

He felt a momentary panic once again, stretching out with his rifle he strained, lifting as high as he could. Drawing the rifle back, he peered into the hole. He could not see daylight.

The snow was packed thickly on top of him. The air had gotten so foul that Dutch could hardly breathe at all. His exertions had used up more oxygen.

Again he attempted it. Standing on the saddle, he held the butt of the rifle in his palm and stretched out his arm as far as possible.

The snow was packed much harder than he would have believed possible. It was an effort to extend his

107

arm. Eventually he felt something give; drawing the rifle back, he peered up through the tunnel he had made. Blue sky—incredibly blue, brilliant. Fresh air wafted down the hole. He drew it into his lungs, feeling momentary relief.

It was only momentary. He realized that he could not dig out of there without smothering himself with falling snow. He sagged down miserably on the saddle, his face turned up to the clear spot of sky.

But even as he watched it, his patch of blue disappeared, smothered by black, rolling clouds. He shook his head, briefly closing his eyes.

The horse nickered and shifted its feet, and Dutch slapped the animal's rump.

"It was a black day when I joined the army, horse. But it's justice, I suppose. Justice. I guess I never told you about that—the killing, I mean."

The horse twisted its head around, looking at the man who was its master—wondering, Dutch supposed, how long they were going to stay locked in this uncomfortable stable.

Remembering, Dutch reaching inside his coat and withdrew one of the thick ham sandwiches. He took a bite, thoughtfully munching on it, and when the horse eyed him mournfully, Dutch tore off a bite, which, surprisingly, the starving horse ate.

"Too much mustard," Dutch grumbled. He sighed and leaned back.

"I don't know. I don't know how I came to be mean, middle-aged, and fat. Yes, I know I'm fat. You're the only one I'd admit it to, though. So don't you blab. How does it happen?" he shook his head.

He had to find a way to get out of there, but none occurred to him. Maybe they would find him. Windy could track over water, they said. Maybe he would come. Dutch swore he would hug that scrawny old coyote if he showed up.

108

But it was unreasonable to think he would—the bastard was probably snoring in the orderly room, his boots propped up on the stove. And Farnsworth was merrily burning the kitchen down...

Maybe the Bestwick boys would find him. Sure—once the captain got the word out that he was missing. They knew which way he would be traveling. The Bestwick boys were horse thieves and whiskey runners, but they would snap up the chance to collect a reward by finding Dutch. And they had a damn good coon hound, too.

Big old redbone hound, lazy as sin until he smelled coon—but Dutch wasn't a coon.

"It's justice," he muttered. "I was going to be a pharmacist, horse. Know that? Other side of the medical business from what I do now, huh? Sawing off a man's legs, arms, crippling him. They never thank me—how can you thank a man for taking off your leg?

"I would have been a pharmacist, too, but for the girl in the yellow dress. Jesus, was that long ago. In another life, Ranger. Got to remember to call you by your name, don't I? No numbers among friends. Ranger.

"God, she was young and full of hot juices. And I was, too. Wild, I was. But not mean—hell, I'm meaner now. I was thin! I mean it. Six feet and one-fifty. One-fifty! Jesus...

"Back then I had no troubles. I could walk in the rain all day and never catch cold. Bumps, bruises, cuts healed up overnight. My teeth were good, my lungs was clean. Now, Jesus, it's carbuncles and gout and hemorrhoids. My body payin' me back for the hard use I've given it."

He lay there trying to recall the girl. Evelyn was her name, but that wasn't how she spelled it. Something funny. Her mother was French, he thought. But he could recall the scent of her, the touch of her bare breasts against his chest, the sweet smell of summer grass, the curve of her hips. But not her face. Not her face anymore.

Only the way the sunlight made golden wires of the hairs on her arms, the way she would run a blade of grass along his lips as he dozed. The distant glitter of sunlight on the mirror of the lake.

"I would have married her, too. Married her and had my own pharmacy. But I found her there. With him. In her father's woodshed. And I went wild. I hit him with a length of cordwood and his head caved in. He just lay there, his pecker hanging out, his head bloody.

"And she was looking at me like I was crazy. Evelyn was naked, but there was nothing attractive about it. Her flesh looked cold, blue. I dropped the wood and turned toward the door and was a mile down the road, straddling my father's mule, before I realized what I had done, before my limbs started shaking, before I had to stop and get down and puke into a ditch.

"I kept riding, but the memory wouldn't stay behind, Ranger. Now I can't recall what Evelyn looked like. But him—I remember him. The caved-in skull, the sad-angry eyes, the pouting little lips, the dark eyes. The poor bastard. Just for wanting a little of what I craved . . . shit! It's justice that I'm here.

"People don't realize what a crime like that does to a man. Waiting for years to hear a tap on the door. Jumping out of your chair when it does come. Skulking away when I see a sheriff, a marshal. It just sits in a man's mind and festers. Me, I'm sour. I wouldn't say it was because of that entirely, but it's like living with some part of you crippled. Christ, Ranger, it's cold!"

He reached for the second sandwich, and then, looking at it, knew he could not eat. He crossed his arms on his chest and took a deep breath, closing his eyes again, aware of the swishing of the horse's tail, the distant shriek of the wind and the faraway cry of a young woman's voice. The face he did not remember, but the scream would always remain etched upon his memory. He shut his eyes more tightly, trying to shut it out, and finally he slept, domed over by tons of snow. Still more snow fell, but Dutch was not aware of that. He simply slept. He slept as he always did, with a heavy weight across his chest, fighting back the demon dreams that tormented him . . . endlessly.

# ten _____

Supply Sergeant Skinflint Wilson was perched on a crate, his eyes wary, as if he were watching a pack of dangerous animals. He looked as though he would like to have a ten-gauge shotgun in his hands to keep the men honest.

"It's not our doing, Sarge," Private MacArthur told him, rolling out his own mattress and blanket, toted over from the enlisted barracks.

Skinflint sat, arms crossed, saying nothing, and Wojensky just shrugged. The captain had decided that the barracks were just too large to heat with the wood available. The storeroom was double-walled and about a third the size of the barracks, and so it was chosen.

"If this goes on for long," Trueblood observed, "Skinflint's going to have a heart attack."

Wilson guarded his goods jealously; he had to. He was caught between the soldier's needs and regimental authority. There was a written form that had to be filled out, even for small items like needles and thread.

Although a soldier was issued everything he needed, down to a pocket comb, upon enlistment, getting replacement articles was damned near impossible. The men resented it at times, especially during inspections. Inspecting officers did not accept excuses. And every item, right down to tent pegs, was required to be lined up properly on display. Yet, after a time in the field, most equipment was a little shabby, worn, or plain missing.

Quartermaster Corps was slow in authorizing equipment, especially to outfits far out in the field, as Outpost Number Nine was. Skinflint, therefore, had developed an almost pathological fear of being looted.

If he thought he could trust any of them, he would undoubtedly have asked the captain for assistance in standing guard. As it was, he looked determined to sit out the entire blizzard, awake and alert on that crate.

In the captain's quarters, things were friendlier if not cozier. The roof continued to leak snowmelt and mud. And the room, now heated to just above the freezing level in order to save fuel, was frosted with the breath of the captain, Sergeant Cohen, Maggie, and Flora. All of them but the captain wore blankets around their shoulders. All of them stayed near the iron stove.

In the BOQ, Fitzgerald and Kincaid shared their fire with Wojensky, Privates Holzer and Yount, and a civilian—Pop Evans, the sutler, who moaned continuously about how much business the blizzard was costing him.

"You miscalculated, you know," Fitzgerald told Evans.

"How's that?" Pop wanted to know.

"Well," Fitzgerald told him, "If you'd had firewood to sell, you plain would have made a killing."

Fitzgerald smiled, but Pop considered it seriously. "You know," he said, "you're right. There might be something to that idea. Maybe I should get some of the

Indians to chop some wood for me."

"If this keeps up," Kincaid said soberly, "we may not have to worry about the next blizzard. This one will be plenty to take care of us."

"You're a bright spot in a cold world," Fitz said.

"I'm getting worried. Have you really looked at our wood supply? I think we're all figuring it'll let up soon and we'll all have a laugh about it. Suppose it doesn't let up? That puts us in a tight spot, wouldn't you say?"

They looked at Matt Kincaid's face in the dull, moving light cast by the iron stove. Fitzgerald lifted his eyes to the window, watching the snow drift steadily downward. Already it was three feet deep across the parade. Nothing moved out there, nothing on all the wide plains.

"The ones I feel for are those men stuck out in it," Fitzgerald said quietly. "This is a piece of cake compared to what they're going through."

Malone lay on his back, quite naked, inside the well-insulated shelter. The twin bonfires outside crackled and cast their heat upon the ice-encrusted circular wall he had built, and in turn, it heated the ingeniously fashioned lean-to and the tent nestled within.

The night had been bitterly cold, and morning was chilly, but inside the small tent it was warm, and Malone lay with one arm behind his head, his eyes closed, feeling the fingers of the woman search the lines of his body.

She was beside him on the floor, naked herself, intrigued with Malone. She studied him with the eyes of an artist, the hands of a passionate woman.

Her fingers ran across his chest, pausing to circle his nipples, to tangle themselves in the dark, curly hair there. She leaned her face to his chest and kissed him.

Elizabeth let her fingers trail downward, across his hard abdomen and along the line of his well-defined thigh muscles. Returning to his crotch, her fingers gently enclosed his half-erect shaft and she leaned her head on his stomach as she toyed with it, lifting it, feeling the slip of the skin, tracing the heavy veins.

Her hand dipped between his legs and cradled his balls. Malone put his hand on her head, feeling the soft warmth of her dark hair, and she kissed his abdomen, her hand closing over his scrotum. His member began to pulse and she returned her attention to it, stroking the underside of it as it lengthened and crept across his belly.

"I *do* have to sketch you," she said. "Before, I was only half serious, but Malone, I do have to draw you."

"Like this?" he asked sleepily.

"Just like this."

He heard her move then, and felt her flesh contact his. She sat straddling him, facing his feet, her arms on his legs, the soft, moist touch of her crotch against his belly, inches from the head of his erection.

She leaned far forward, gripping Malone's toes. Her hair brushed his shins as she kissed both of his knees. Then she straightened slowly, her hands running up his legs to rest on his thighs.

Malone lifted one eyelid lazily, studying her slim back, the flare of her buttocks. As he watched, she lifted herself slightly and he felt her slide up on his erect sex.

She did not slip him inside immediately, but slid along the underside of his member, her head thrown back, hands massaging his thighs.

She moved only a few inches, forward and back, smearing herself against Malone, building herself slowly toward a sensual peak.

She stopped then, and Malone felt her lift her hips and slide him inside her. She was warm, damp, ready. He let his hands drop to her buttocks, and his palms rested on her smooth flesh as she lifted herself rhythmically, looking back between her legs to watch Malone's shaft sliding in and out of her, watching his peaceful face beyond.

She settled on him, sitting upright. She tossed her head so that her hair fell across her back, and with her fingers she reached down, exploring herself and Malone

116

simultaneously. He felt her shudder, saw her arms moving more intently as her fingers worked against her own demanding flesh, against his throbbing shaft.

Then she came, suddenly, exquisitely, and collapsed against Malone, gripping his legs tightly, her hair falling across his feet.

He held himself back, although his loins ached. Opening his eyes now, he could see the moon of her buttocks, the pinkness of her cleft where he entered her, the small, tangled hairs.

He caressed her thighs, her hips, and she turned, rolling to him, kissing him with a searching, hungry mouth as her hands gripped his shoulders.

Elizabeth rolled off him now, and lay facing him on the small bed of blankets and pine boughs. Her eyes sparkled as Malone touched her face with his rough hands, cupped her full, nearly round breasts. She scooted to him, her hands on his chest. Kissing him again, she rolled onto her stomach, and Malone let his fingers roam, let his lips kiss her white shoulder, her back, the swell of her buttocks.

Getting to his knees, he scooted down and straddled her, letting the length of his shaft rest in the cleft between her buttocks. Elizabeth's hands reached back and pressed him into the crease more deeply, holding him there with a slight pressure of her fingertips as he rocked back and forth, watching her white fingers against the dark ruddiness of his own flesh.

He continued to sway against her, knowing that he could not hold back his orgasm much longer, did not want to. Her buttocks encased him, that fine white flesh flexing as she clenched her muscles.

Abruptly she took charge, reaching beneath her to grip his shaft, lifting her hips, sliding him deep within her, her fingers scratching at his scrotum, trying for a hold that was difficult to achieve as Malone began rocking against her in earnest, watching the rise and fall of her hips as he slid deeply into her, his shaft glossy with

117

the honey of her body, pulsing with need.

She moaned faintly, distantly, and inched upward until she was on her knees and Malone was kneeling behind her, his hands clutching for her pendant breasts, his motion furious, urgent.

He knelt upright, reached between her legs, and spread her, finding her damp fingers, which intertwined with his own and spread her fully as Malone, plunged to the hilt, came deeply, twitching, thrusting as Elizabeth found his balls and held them to her.

Her own breathing was ragged, her hands demanding. Her mouth was open as if in pain, the white of her teeth showing. She rolled over abruptly, holding Malone in place, and hugged him tightly with her arms and legs, which wrapped around him as she began anew, swaying, rolling, kissing his neck, biting at his shoulders.

Her hands dropped to his ass, clutching him, tearing at him, and they rocked together, her breasts pressed against his chest, their bodies slick with perspiration now, heated by their efforts.

Elizabeth panted. Small, nearly childish sounds escaped from her throat with each thrust. Tiny sloshing sounds emerged from her womb as Malone, intent, rising to a second climax, pounded his pelvis against hers.

She grunted and clawed at his buttocks, her entire body going stiff as her voice sounded tiny chirps with every exhalation, until finally she shrieked—a muffled, exhausted, fulfilled shriek that she shut off by jamming her fisted knuckles into her mouth. She bit at her knuckles and, after a frantic burst of driving effort, fell completely limp.

Flat on her back, her legs opened to the maximum, she lay utterly still as Malone, without motion, came again with a slow, extended pulsing that drained his loins and left him in limp exhaustion.

"Now," she said. "Now is when I'd like to draw you. The way your face glows, the peacefulness of it."

"Draw away," Malone said panting. "For myself, I'm resting."

"Do rest," she said. "For later. For myself..." Her voice trailed away into a gigantic yawn and they slept, wrapped in each other's arms. Outside, unseen, the snow continued to fall.

The wind was effectively blunted within the rising walls of Arapaho Canyon, but Windy, who had ridden out at dawn, returned to report.

"We're snowed in for a time. There's fifteen feet of snow at the entrance to the canyon."

Windy spat into the fire, squatted, and poured himself some coffee out of the gallon pot there.

"How are the cattle doing, Childes?" Olsen asked the trail boss.

The man nodded with bleak satisfaction. "All right. They're not exactly getting fat, but as far as I know, there's only been three die off on us."

"Then the agency will get its beef." Gus Olsen looked around at the bleak, white landscape. The mottled clouds tossed and frothed overhead, the trees quivered in the wind. "Provided, of course, this damned blizzard ever lets up."

"I wish there was some way to get word to the agency," Childes said.

"Well," Windy said over his coffee, "there ain't. One thing, though. The Indians may be restless about not getting their ration of beef, but they're damned sure not going to cause much trouble over it."

"Not in this weather," Gus agreed.

"How far is it to the agency, once it does clear?" Childes wanted to know.

"No more'n a day," Windy answered immediately. "Well, a day without snow. In this, maybe a day and a half."

"Good. If the agent can hold the Indians' mood down, everything should work out. Figure on staying to watch the issue?" Childes asked.

"No." Gus shook his head. He would like to; it was

119

quite a show. There being no opportunity to hunt buffalo, the steers were issued one at a time, and the Cheyenne, allowed to pursue them on their ponies, brought them down with arrows as if it were a buffalo hunt.

There were always quite a few onlookers. It was a day of celebration for the Cheyenne, and as good a day as any for getting drunk and dancing for the white settlers.

Gathered on the hillsides around the agency, they would watch as the Indians, stripped to breechclouts, themselves and their horses painted, charged down the slopes, pursuing the panicked steers.

After bringing one down, a brave would wheel his horse around and ride victoriously homeward. After a time the squaws and kids would trail down to skin and butcher the cattle.

From time to time it got a little exciting. The Cheyenne warriors were worked up, painted, and armed. In the early years, troopers were usually positioned around the agency to head off any exuberant spirits.

Now it was generally less hectic, but still quite a show to those who had never seen it. Olsen had seen it a number of times. But the captain would be wanting them back at the outpost.

At the sound of a loud crack, the three men's heads came around as one. The cowboys and soldiers had tied lassos onto the great dead sycamore and tugged, toppling it. As it hit the ground it broke itself into firewood, settling after a single bounce into the snow.

With the cook's ax and bowie knives, the men got to work on the tree. Camden Shoate had the ax and he was concentrating on his work. Chip by chip, he cut a wedge into the white meat of the sycamore log.

He worked evenly, but not too quickly. Breaking into a sweat that would freeze next to his skin could be dangerous. Stopping to take a deep, cold breath, he watched the low clouds scud past over the willow-rife bluffs across the frozen river.

From the corner of his eye he saw a familiar face. His

jaw twitched and his hands tightened their grip on the curved ax handle.

McBride had a length of wood standing on end, his bowie blade sunk into the end of the log. With a rock he hammered down on the top edge of the knife, using it for a wedge. The dry sycamore wood split easily into halves.

McBride looked directly at Shoate as he turned one half to halve it again. His eyes were dark and savage, and he was smiling. But it was a taunting smile, and Shoate glanced around. There was one soldier at the root end of the tree, far away. Everyone else was carrying wood to the fire.

"Guess what I'm thinking, Shoate?" McBride asked in a hiss. He drove the fist-sized rock in his hand against the blade of his knife. The log split down its length on the first blow. "Thinking of three good men that got killed because of one drunk deserter."

"McBride, look, I—"

"Thinking of that man," McBride went on as he glanced at the camp himself, picked up the other half-log, and split it. "Thinking that this should be his head. That would be a kind of justice, wouldn't it?"

"Knock it off, McBride," Shoate said, his face twisting with anger. "Your sergeant ordered you to stay away from me."

"Sure." McBride grinned. "And I always follow orders. Didn't you, when you were a soldier? Didn't you, when you were posted, told to stay alert?"

McBride hefted another log and split it. Savagely, violently. He lifted his eyes to Shoate triumphantly. "Splits clean, doesn't it? This is a damned fine knife." He held it up and Shoate glanced at it, fascinated despite the shudder which ran along his spine.

"Stop it!"

"Of course, I'll have to put a new edge on it. It takes a fine edge, Shoate. I've shaved with it. He turned the knife over, and Shoate studied the curve of the blade,

121

the deep "blood groove" ground into the flat of the knife.

"You're crazy, McBride!" Shoate looked around desperately, searching for help. Jenkins and the others had halted their work for a cup of coffee at the fire. What did McBride want? To goad him into attacking first? Lift the ax and go for him?

And then what? A murder charge, pure and simple. Shoate slammed his ax into the tree trunk, walking away as quickly as he could.

McBride's taunt followed him: "Go on! Git! You can run. You can run, but you can't hide. Not now, Shoate."

Private Grayson, who had been working nearest Reb, sauntered over toward him and asked, lifting his chin, "What was that?"

"What?" Reb asked innocently. "Him? Search me. I think he wasn't feeling too well."

Grayson took off his hat and scratched his head, frowning at McBride, but no more information was forthcoming. Grayson shrugged and got back to work, watching Reb, who puckered his lips and appeared to be whistling as he worked, although Grayson could hear nothing above the constant wind.

Shoate tramped to the fire, asked for coffee, and was poured a cup, which he took with a trembling hand. Childes noticed it and asked his hand, "What's up, Camden?"

"Nothin'," Shoate growled. "Damned cold is all."

And Shoate was trembling, but Childes had been over the plains and up the mountains, and he knew that Camden Shoate was shaking with anger and not from the cold.

"Want me to put a lid on this?" Childes asked.

"On what?" Shoate demanded hotly. "Why's everybody jumping on my wagon all of a sudden?"

"Just thought something was wrong," Childes said, taken aback.

"Sure, something's wrong. It's damned cold, and we're squatting up the fucking canyon with a herd of cows."

122

Childes knew enough not to press it. Nodding slightly, he returned to the fire. Shoate started to drink his coffee, but changed his mind and threw it into the fire, where it hissed angrily.

Then he stomped away, making deep tracks through the snow. He circled the chuckwagon and stood next to it, near the water barrel, which had frozen and popped its staves. He clenched his fists and looked darkly at the high-rising canyon walls, feeling the wind against his face.

Then, turning, Shoate leaned his hand against the rough planking of the chuckwagon, closing his eyes tightly, his shoulders rolling with emotion.

He skipped supper, standing on the fringe of the fire-light, his collar turned up, hat tugged down. He could see McBride clearly, although he was almost certain McBride could not see him.

Reb laughed and yarned with the men, at one point throwing out his hands in an expressive gesture, which, combined with whatever he had said, broke the gathered cowboys and soldiers into laughter.

It was funny, but Shoate recalled now that he had always liked this rangy Texan, wanted to hang around him. McBride had been several years older and already army-wise when Shoate signed on.

He stood looking at McBride, watching the fire burnish his face. Then, slowly, Shoate turned and walked off alone into the snow-filled night.

Away from the fire, the snow seemed to glisten with a radiance of its own. Blue-white, it lay humped and rifted across the canyon floor. A miserable steer lowed its displeasure with this cold night, and beyond the herd Shoate caught a faint glimpse of the night herder, moving in a slow circle around the cattle.

McBride hit him without warning, slamming into Shoate's back, his shoulder jarring into the cowboy's spine.

Shoate's head snapped back and his boots went out from under him as they toppled to the snow. Shoate kicked out desperately at McBride, who had turned him and now straddled him.

But it was useless. McBride was the bigger of the two, and the angrier. He sat on Shoate's chest and crushed a right hook into Shoate's jaw, driving his head into the snow.

Shoate struck back. A straight left glanced off Reb's ear, and McBride shook it off. He lifted his right again, and again slammed it into Shoate's face.

Shoate felt the hot blood trickle from his nostrils, felt the dizziness begin inside his skull. Lights flickered and his ears rang, and McBride hit him again.

Out of desperation, Shoate rose, bucking, arching his back, clawing at Reb to free himself. Then he got to his feet, trying to make a run for it. Reb caught him by the belt and dragged him down again, mauling him like a big cat.

"Get off, get off...damn you!" McBride shoved down on the back of Shoate's head, pushing his face into the snow. Shoate wriggled and gasped. There was a real danger of suffocating in the snow, but McBride just didn't give a damn whether Shoate suffocated or not.

Shoate bucked wildly, trying to shake the man off his back. Getting to hands and knees, with McBride riding him like a wild bull, he managed to roll over and, clawing at McBride's face, to free himself.

He stood, arms dangling limply, to face Reb, who was panting with wild emotion.

"Listen, McBride—" Shoate gasped.

But McBride wasn't listening. He lowered his head and charged, his skull impacting painfully against Shoate's chest. McBride butted upward and cracked his skull against Shoate's jaw, clacking his teeth together.

Again they went down, both men windmilling punches. McBride's were by far the more telling. Shoate collapsed against the snow, unmoving. His right eye was swollen, his cheek split, and his mouth leaked blood.

McBride got to his knees and then stood, beckoning to Shoate.

'Get up, boy, I'm not done."

"I can't get up." Shoate choked and fell into a cough-ing spasm. In the middle of it, McBride leaned over and, closing a fist, gripped Shoate's coat, pulling him up.

"Get your butt up, boy!" McBride snarled. "I'm not half done."

"Goddamm it! When will you be through? When I'm dead?"

McBride's lips formed into a tight smile. "Three good men are already dead."

"You don't know how it was," Shoate gasped. McBride let go of his coat front, and he fell back against the snow.

"No? Why don't you tell me, then?"

"I will." Shoate rolled onto his side and spat out a mouthful of blood. "I never talked to nobody about it, but I will now."

"No big song and dance, Shoate," Reb said, glancing toward the campfire. "You got something to say, out with it. You got something to say that'll convince me yo' weren't a damned drunken deserter who cost three good men their lives, let's hear it."

"I can't convince you of nothing, McBride. But I'll tell you. I'll tell you," he repeated, nodding his head heavily.

"That was my first patrol. The Kiowa were raising hell. Remember that butchered-up family we found at Stockton Corners?"

Reb nodded, and Shoate went on:

"Turned my guts, Reb. I drew burial detail. I kept looking at the woman. So mutilated you couldn't tell if she'd been pretty or not. She was just carved-up meat. They cut her arms and stripped the meat away—she must have still been alive. God! I thought of it for days.

"Suddenly we were in Kiowa country, and we knew it. I had night guard. Corporal Bird wandered over and offered me a bottle to keep the chill away."

"Bird wouldn't have done that." Bird was one of the men killed by the Kiowa.

"If you don't want to believe that, don't. But I had

125

whiskey and I had night guard. And they were out there."
Shoate's voice dropped to a whisper. "I knew they were
out there. I could feel it. When I heard a nighthawk
shriek, I nearly jumped out of my skin. God—I took a
drink, a deep drink that nearly turned my guts. It filled
me up with fire, turned my eyes to watering."

"And you kept on drinking."

"Yes, dammit! I kept on drinking. It was my first time
out, Reb. Christ, I was only eighteen. And I kept seeing
that butchered family. I drank, but it didn't help. I knew
they were out there, knew they were coming to get me.
To torture me. I got drunker. Drunk as I could. My knees
wobbled and I couldn't tell if it was the liquor or fear.
I heard something in the brush and I finished the bottle.
I tried to lift my rifle, but it was heavy in my hands,
shaking.

"God, McBride," Shoate pleaded. His voice broke.
"I was scared enough to shit my pants. I was drunk. I
told myself I was no coward. No coward, but I was. And
the idea came to me—" Shoate's voice was throttled
with emotion. Tears streamed down his battered face.
He snuffed and finished, "I got on my damn horse and
I rode! I rode until the horse was foundering, and then
I walked. And I kept on walking.

"Later I heard about it—the massacre. I was drunk
for a month. That thought rode with me, McBride. I was
a *coward*. Men had died because of me! Do you know
how that feels? I was nothing. A coward. A deserter. A
murderer!" Shoate's face was the color of putty. His
Adam's apple jerked up and down and he turned his head
away, sobbing against his arm. "God, McBride," he said
in a muffled voice, "you're a soldier. Haven't you ever
been scared? Haven't you?"

McBride stood. Looking into the distance, he sucked
in a deep breath. Shoate's body quivered with the sobbing. McBride answered.

"Yeah, I guess I have."

He felt suddenly like putting a hand on Shoate's shoulder, but he couldn't bring himself to do it. He was looking at a tragic, broken man, and he both despised and pitied him.

He turned on his heel and walked back toward the camp. The fire flickered on the snow, smearing it crimson and gold. Behind him, the bawling cattle covered the pathetic sounds of a man's sobbing.

# *eleven* ──────────

No one answered Matt Kincaid's knock on the door. No one could hear it over the howling of the wind. Snow swept steadily down. The barracks across the parade were completely obscured. Matt swung the door open and entered the dark, cold room, bringing with him a swirl of snow.

Flora Conway looked around. The wind toyed with her hair. She wore a heavy coat, and had a muffler wrapped around her throat. Warner Conway, next to the stove, glanced at Matt with a grim smile.

"Sir." Kincaid nodded first to the captain and then to Sergeant Cohen, who sat shuffling papers with gloved hands.

"What is it, Matt?" Conway asked.

"I'll get right to the point," Kincaid said, moving to the stove, rubbing his hands. "I want to take a volunteer party out after firewood."

"In this?" Flora Conway exclaimed with distress.

"In this, if I have to. Otherwise, ma'am, we're going to be in poor shape tonight. BOQ is out of wood." He glanced at the Conways' own depleted supply. "We'll have nothing to burn but the walls by tomorrow — and they're probably too wet," he added.

"Just how, Matt, do you intend to do this?" Captain Conway had to be pragmatic. "The snow is up to a horse's shoulder. A man can't walk through it. Where's the nearest wood? Willow Ford? That's a good mile and a half."

"It is." Matt was determined, his jaw set. He didn't need Conway to tell him what the risks were. He had spent half the night turning it over in his mind, convincing himself it was impossible, knowing that it needed to be done if they were to survive.

Captain Conway sighed and turned his eyes away. "Go ahead, Matt. Volunteers only."

Flora looked at him sharply, with deep concern. It was nothing less than suicide — he couldn't let Kincaid go out! But she said nothing.

"Then I'm one of your volunteers," Ben Cohen said, rising from his chair.

Conway looked at Maggie Cohen, who had gone pale. "No, you're not," the captain said sternly. He added, "I need my first shirt here."

Ben Cohen felt like arguing, but a man doesn't argue with his CO. Disappointed, he sat down again, saying, "Good luck, Matt."

Kincaid nodded. His face was tense. The snow on his shoulders was melting slowly. "I'd better go, before I change my mind," he said.

Back in the bachelor officers' quarters, he explained what he meant to do. Fitzgerald was ready to go, but Matt told the second lieutenant, "I think one officer on the mission is plenty, Fitz."

"Well, I'm going," Corporal Wojensky said, standing up.

"All right. I appreciate it, Corporal."

130

"Me." Wolfgang Holzer stood in the corner and bowed stiffly.

"Do you understand what this mission is, Holzer? We're going for wood—out there!" Kincaid wasn't sure Holzer knew what he was volunteering for, but the private nodded again.

"Oh, sure. Wood."

Kincaid nodded. "We'll need a man or two more, Wojensky. Make your way down to the supply room and see if you can scrape up some volunteers."

"Yes, sir," Wojensky buttoned up his coat and opened the door. He was surprised to find Holzer beside him. "You don't have to go with me now."

Holzer grinned and shook his head. Shrugging, Wojensky went out into the blast of the wind. Struggling through the drifts along the boardwalk, they made their way to supply.

The place looked like a refugee camp. Men, fully dressed, wore every piece of clothing they owned. The fire barely burned in the iron stove. MacArthur was cramming it full of odds and ends. Some of Skinflint's shelving seemed to be missing and he stood, arms crossed, guarding the rest.

"Anybody want to take a walk?" Wojensky asked. He got a murmured negative chorus in response.

"For wood?" MacArthur asked.

"That's right."

"I'll go. Might as well freeze out there, doing something, as sitting here."

Unnoticed, Holzer had walked across the room as they entered. Now, at the crash, Wojensky looked up sharply. Sergeant Wilson was apoplectic.

"What in God's name are you doing!" he shrieked.

Holzer looked around with a grin. He had a hammer in his hand and was methodically dismantling a barrel. He struck the bands once more and the barrel collapsed, spilling its contents, a few pounds of nails.

131

"You idiot!" Skinflint wailed. Wojensky put his hand on the sergeant's arm.

"Wait. He's got something in mind."

And he did. As they watched, Holzer picked up two of the wide staves and set them on the floor, parallel. Then he placed his feet on them and stood there grinning.

"He's crazy," Skinflint Wilson moaned.

"No, I don't think so. Go on, Holzer."

Holzer did so. Stepping to the harnesses that hung on the wall, he selected one piece, which he cut with his pocket knife. Skinflint gasped.

"Jesus! That took me four months to get."

But Holzer paid no attention. Returning to the staves, he crouched down, and with the spilled nails he began building something, tacking the harness to the barrel staves.

"Flaming crazy!" Wilson muttered, rubbing his head. "And you're crazy to let him do it, Wojensky!"

"No. He's not crazy, and I'm not either," Wojensky said. "Don't you see what he's got?"

Skinflint looked with sour interest at the soldier who now stood balanced on the barrel staves, straps around his ankles, taking a few tentative steps.

"Yeah," Skinflint said. "He's got sticks tied to his damned boots."

"He's got *snowshoes*. Norwegian snowshoes, Sergeant. I've seen them a time or two. In Germany I guess it's a more common sight. Those are what Snowshoe Johnson used to deliver mail over the Sierras in winter, over forty-foot drifts. You're a genius, Holzer!"

Holzer smiled and nodded, and got immediately to work on a second pair of skis. MacArthur, who had been watching closely, got down on one knee and started duplicating Holzer's efforts.

Lieutenant Kincaid was as skeptical as Wilson had been. Unlike Wilson, he had heard of skis, but he looked dubiously at Holzer's improvisation.

132

"We haven't got much to lose, sir," Wojensky told him. "We know what the result's going to be afoot. We'll be slogging it every step of the way."

"All right. Let's try it," Matt agreed.

Holzer wore his skis inside the room, and he switched his feet from side to side with practiced ease. He had two broom handles, and with these he was able to swivel fluidly.

Kincaid himself was clumsy and still doubtful when he got to his feet, the barrel-stave snowshoes strapped to his boots.

"Let's try it. As you say, we've got nothing to lose."

Each man had a gunnysack for firewood with him as they stepped outside. The wind had finally abated a little, but the snow was deep as far as the eye could see.

Holzer stepped off the plank walk and onto the parade. With a grin, he demonstrated a gliding gait that took him quickly around in a tight circle, ending before the lieutenant, who shook his head.

"If we can all do that well . . ."

It wasn't as easy as Holzer made it look. Kincaid went down twice within half a minute. But finally, balancing precariously, they managed to get to the front gate, and beneath the flabbergasted stare of the half-frozen gate guard, they moved out onto the prairie.

It was slow going, but their feet did not sink into the snow mass. The sky was a gray, swirling thing, the land gray-white, humped, and desolate.

By the time they had covered half a mile, MacArthur seemed to have gotten the hang of it. He moved out ahead with Holzer, and the two enlisted men were forced, time and again, to wait for the others.

Willow Ford lay gray against gray. Broken, denuded trees sprung up from the snow. Kincaid was winded by the time they reached it, but he did not take time to rest.

"Let's get what we can while the weather holds," he ordered. A huge bank of clouds loomed to the north, dark as ink, bringing more snow.

Hurriedly they got to it, breaking dead branches, stuffing their gunnysacks with all they could carry. They were gone and skiing across the flats before the snows hit. It was only now that Kincaid began to get the idea. Even with the heavy sack slung over his shoulder, he was able to glide for quite a ways with very little effort. Before, he had taken each step cautiously, not letting the skis work for him. Now he smiled as he scudded down a shallow slope.

Holzer was beside him, grinning, and Kincaid gave him the thumbs-up. If there was time, he decided, they might even make another trip to the ford. This time it would be quicker.

Now, looking to the skies, Kincaid saw something that lifted his spitits. Far to the north, beyond the bank of black clouds, he saw a definite, clear patch of blue.

He pointed it out to Wojensky, who grinned with relief. With the wood they were bringing in, they would last this night, no matter what the storm clouds offered. And tomorrow—damned if it didn't look like it might be over. Maybe this big blizzard had blown itself out.

It was the dead of night when Dutch awoke. His teeth chattered violently. He was cold and ravenously hungry, but that was not what had awakened him.

"What'd you do, horse? Hit me with your tail again?" He thought then how sick he was of looking at the tail end of that damned bay horse. Still wondering what had awakened him, he got the answer.

A drop of water splashed against his face. He pawed it away angrily and then straightened up with sudden understanding. Cold he was, inside this icy tomb, but outside it must be warming.

Putting his eye to his airhole, he could see the black sky above. And there, twinkling like a shiny promise, a silver star.

Water trickled down the airhole and into his face once more, but he hardly felt it. If it was warmer tonight, why, by morning it would be downright pleasant. Outside.

Outside—but he was inside, trapped in an icy prison of his own making. With a sudden surge of emotion that approached panic, Rothausen realized that the thaw, if thaw there was, might release the lock that the cold had clamped on the snow above him and send it tumbling down.

He was probably making a great deal out of nothing. After all, it had cleared before during the blizzard, then darkened over again, and the snows had come with renewed fury.

He peered steadily out of his airhole, seeing a second star, then a third. There was little wind, he was certain of that. If there had been wind, the light snow would be drifting past, clouding his view, and such was not the case.

"We'll see in the morning, Ranger. See if it holds. If we see that damned yellow sun!" He rubbed his hands with warm glee. "Then what?" he asked, his old pessimism returning. "Then what?"

Dutch sat down on the saddle, reaching again for the second sandwich, forgetting that he had eaten it the day before. His stomach rumbled its protest, and he silenced it by falling off to a troubled sleep.

When he awoke, there was a regular trickle of water running down his breathing hole and onto his back, soaking him to the skin.

He clawed his red-rimmed eyes apart and went to the hole, peering up. Clear blue sky! It dazzled his eye, but he stayed there, fascinated by the sight. There was not a wisp of cloud visible. He drew back, wiping his eye, convincing himself that it was snowmelt running down his cheek.

"And now what, horse?" Dutch asked the bay. "If we were out there, we'd have a chance. Maybe our only chance. For all I know, there's another blizzard coming in."

The horse pricked up its ears, but could offer no advice. Dutch slammed his fist into his palm repeatedly. Glancing up at his blanket, knowing tons of snow were

135

melting overhead, he felt a deep pessimism.

If he waited for the melt, he would likely smother. What if he didn't wait, but made his try? Above, he knew there was six to eight feet of snow, ready to collapse.

"What about straight ahead, the direction you're pointed? The way we came in?" he asked the horse.

That too was a gamble, but it seemed that the time for rolling the dice had come. To sit and wait was to die. From suffocation, hunger, or freezing.

He tried to ease around the horse, but in the narrow crevice it was impossible. Dropping to his hands and knees, Dutch crawled forward beneath it.

He dug tentatively at the snow that had avalanched over the entrance that first night. It crumbled away and he took an involuntary step back as á large chunk fell at his feet.

"Need a damned shovel, is what I need. Either that, or..."

He looked at Ranger, looked him directly in the eye. "How about you, you dogmeat, you?"

He looked at the snowbank, and then again at the horse. It was a wild idea, and if he was wrong, he would not get a second chance.

"Hell, let's try it. I'm gettin' all claustrophoby in here."

With sudden resolve, Dutch threw his saddle over the horse's back and cinched up. The bay looked expectantly, uneasily at Rothausen.

"We're through sitting. There's clean air and sunlight outside. You ready?" he asked. Then he added, "Me neither."

But he took a deep breath and rolled into the saddle. His shoulders touched the sagging blanket as he did so. He whispered, "You ain't gonna like this."

"Heeyah!" Rothausen shouted, and dug into the bay's flanks with his boot heels.

The bay, startled by the action, lunged forward, panicked and amazed. Ranger hit the snowbank on the second leap, and Dutch gripped the horse's neck, neglecting the reins.

He spurred the horse again, and it dove into the snow, which broke free, slamming against Dutch's head and shoulders, sending his hat spinning off, slapping his cheeks and hands with hard, icy fingers.

Ice collapsed on him, and he was nearly knocked from the bay's back, but he held determinedly to the horse's neck and spurred again. The hesitant, panicked animal leaped forward again, and this time they broke free.

Free, out into the cold, clear light of day, as the snow from the bank above and behind them creaked and grumbled loose, filling the crevice as Dutch rode the horse free in a frothing avalanche.

He rode thirty feet, still clinging only to the horse's neck. Turning back, he saw the snow being sucked into the vacuum of the pit, saw it shift and settle. Then, shakily, he got down from the saddle, and leaning his head against the horse's neck, he hugged it, his eyes closed tightly.

"Let's get on home," he said. The sun was piercing. He could barely see as it glistened off the miles and miles of new snow.

He patted the still-wary horse's neck and stepped again into the saddle, gathering up the reins. Then, with a nudge of his knees, he set the bay to a slow walk through the deep, glistening snow.

The going was rough. The horse was weak from hunger and the snow was deep. Rothausen was in high spirits, but his head spun and he felt weak. His stomach rumbled, reminding him of how little he had eaten in the last three days.

Emerging from the canyon mouth and onto the long plains, he could see just how difficult the trip back to Number Nine was going to be. The drifts were five feet high and more.

The bay was already trembling with weariness, and

Dutch felt little better. He had to make an effort to stay in the saddle.

It came to him.

"The Bestwick place. The boys will have food and hay—they keep plenty of hay on hand, what with the number of horses that are on and off their place."

Hesitating only briefly, Dutch swung the horse that way. The Bestwick place was much nearer than Outpost Number Nine. After a good meal and a little rest, with a fresher horse under him, the return ride would be a piece of cake.

He swung north and then west along the frozen Littletree Creek. The Bestwick place was at the fork in the river, set back among a stand of oaks. He had found it by noon.

"There," he told the horse. "See that? That means hay for you."

He was only half a mile from the low, gray soddy, but it took almost an hour to get there, through drifts that sometimes reached the horse's chest. When he finally swung down in the snow-covered yard, he had a sudden fear that perhaps the boys weren't around. But there were horses in the corral. Miserable, long-haired, they looked at Rothausen.

No one looked out, and the hound wasn't there to yap and howl. Dutch frowned and walked wearily around the house. There were footprints leading to the back door, and he tapped at it.

After a minute, Tom Bestwick appeared at a window, gun in hand, cautiously peering through the shabby curtains. The door opened a minute later.

"How do, Sergeant. Bad time for riding."

Bestwick's eyes searched the land beyond Rothausen. Then, apparently satisfied, he holstered his gun and stepped out. "What can I do for you?"

"I'd like some feed for my horse," Dutch explained. "We were caught up in the hills during the blizzard. Poor fellow's 'most gaunted."

Tom Bestwick looked the bay over with an expert's

eye, and nodded. "We got hay."

Bestwick pointed out the lean-to shelter where the hay was kept, and Dutch led Ranger to it. Forking out some green hay, he added two scoops of some oats he found in a bin.

Then he rubbed the horse down. Leaving it, he walked back to the house, where Tom Bestwick waited, his thumbs thrust in his belt.

"I don't reckon you could feed a hungry man as well?"

Bestwick nodded. "Come on in."

His brother sat at the kitchen table, stockinged, his filthy feet propped up on the rough plank table. "There's stew in the pot," Tom Bestwick told him. "It ain't hot, but you're welcome to it."

Dutch served himself from the black iron pot. With a bent spoon, he emptied the wooden bowlful of stew that he had dished out, as the Bestwick boys watched.

"Fill it again, if you like," Tom told him.

Dutch did, with thanks. Now, eating more slowly, he had time to examine what he was eating. Old carrots and greens, some tender, oddly flavored meat, and dark, floury gravy.

"You know, boys, I'm a cook. But damned if anything I've ever made tasted as good to me as that did. You've saved my life, I reckon."

Tom waved a hand. "Nothin'." Then he rolled a smoke and offered the fixings to Dutch, who made his own cigarette and leaned back in the rough wooden chair, fully satisfied.

"All the same," he said, pointing a finger, "you boys ever want a meal—anytime, day or night—you come see me at Number Nine."

"We'll do that," Tom agreed.

"By the way," Dutch asked, looking around, "where's that hound dog of yours?"

Tom Bestwick looked at his brother and cleared his throat. "Passed on, Sergeant. It's been hard weather around here."

"Oh, too bad."

139

The Bestwick boys exchanged a glance and then looked at the floor. It came to Dutch then, suddenly. He looked at them closely, then at the pot, and finally at the empty bowl on the table.

"He . . . passed on?"

"Quite sudden," Tom Bestwick said without looking at Dutch.

"Yeah." Rothausen looked again at the bowl, at the pot of stew. He saw the dog's collar hanging on a nail near the door, but he didn't ask. He decided he really didn't want to know.

He had planned on resting up for a few hours, but suddenly he had a strong impulse to get out of there. He saddled his horse and rode from the yard and out onto the prairie. The Bestwick boys stood on the front porch and watched him go, a hungry expression in their dark eyes.

# twelve _____

Dawn had been brilliant in the mountains. The coming sun had flooded the snowy flanks of the high peaks with crimson and gold. In the valleys, a deep purple flush colored the land.

The sky was crystal clear as far as the eye could see, and the breeze off the peaks far above was light and fresh.

Malone stood looking past the timber toward the distant flats, and he nodded to himself. Returning to the tent, he told Elizabeth, "It's time to go."

"To go?" She looked up from the bed, her eyes dazed with sleep, her dark hair rumpled, her gown loosely tied, revealing one smooth white shoulder.

"Yes. The weather's broken. I think we'd better have a try at it."

"Not up that dreadful mountain trail again?" she asked in near panic.

"No. That's where the snow will have been the heaviest. There's no need to follow that ridge trail unless we want to go over the range. And we definitely do not. I think we can make it out by going the way Chapel went."

"And David! You think he might have made it?"

"He might have," Malone answered with a smile. After all, anything was possible. That seemed to liven Elizabeth up a little. ·

She popped from the bed, hurried to Malone, hugged him, and started getting dressed. He went out into the brilliant sunlight and began making up a pack.

Half an hour later they were ready to go.

"Malone?" Elizabeth said.

He turned, looking questioningly at her.

"I have something for you." She walked forward, hands behind her back. She held out a piece of paper.

"What's this?" he asked.

"Look and see."

He did, unrolling the paper, which was a receipt from the sutler at Fort Laramie. Turning it over, Malone found a sketch of himself, done in charcoal.

"I did it while you were sitting at the fire one night. Do you like it?"

"I like it fine—sorry I'm such a homely subject," Malone answered. "Thank you."

He rolled it again and tucked it into his pack. Shouldering the pack, he turned and looked over the camp. Then, nodding, he led off down the long, snow-deep slopes toward the distant prairie.

The sun shone brightly. Ice balls, where snow had melted and refrozen, glittered like crystal on the trees. The scent of pine was heavy in the cold air. Long ranks of blue spruce and occasional cedar lined out toward the valley below.

The snow was heavy, but by staying in the woods, they were able to make decent time. At least it was downhill, Malone thought gratefully.

They pulled up once, suddenly, and Malone held Elizabeth back. Silently he pointed out a huge silvertip grizzly waddling across the snowfields. Awakened by hunger, the bear was on the prowl. It was the worst possible time to run into a bear, and they held their position, hardly breathing, until it ambled across the winding, icy creek and disappeared into the forest beyond.

They walked the next mile quickly, keeping to the spruce woods. At noon, weary and hungry, they snacked on jerky and stale, dry biscuits. They drank water from the creek, which was fringed with ice on either side. The water was so cold it made their teeth ache, but it was sweet, revitalizing.

Elizabeth lay back for a few minutes on a sun-warmed rock, gazing into the crystal skies, where a pair of glossy crows wheeled and scolded.

Malone kept an eye on the northern horizon, but the weather seemed to be holding.

It was already late afternoon, the sun winking through the trees on the western slopes, when they came to a bluff. It was thirty feet to the flats below, and Malone, casting back and forth, was unable to find an easy way down.

The creek fanned out into a thin waterfall there, and where it hit the rocks below, the late sunlight formed a rainbow above the icy banks.

"It's down and over, seems like," Malone said.

"It looks dangerous," she answered, and he nodded.

"It is, but not so bad, I don't think. Besides, there's no choice."

Elizabeth sat down on the edge of the bluff, warily eyeing the sharp drop, the snow beneath.

"Have at it, woman," Malone said, and over she went.

She slid down the bluff in a flurry of snow, and landed sharply in the drift below. She was slow in getting up, but get up she did, rubbing her bustle. Malone followed.

"Well," she said, as he rose, dusting himself, "that was nearly fun."

"Want to go up and do it again?"

"No." She smiled. "I did say *nearly*."

"Stand here a minute, will you?" Malone asked. Elizabeth frowned in puzzlement and nodded. There was something Malone had seen from above that he wanted to check, something that didn't belong—a patch of color against the white of the ice and snow.

He walked toward the creek, glancing up at the sheet of water the falls produced. Then, walking downstream a few yards, he found it.

He crouched down and dug the snow away with his hands. Shaking his head, he covered it up again. He turned to see Elizabeth above him, her hands to her mouth.

"It's David, isn't it?"

"It's David," he confirmed.

Malone got to his feet and walked to her. He held her as the mist from the falls swept over them, as the shadows crept out from under the trees. The roar of the waterfall was in his ears, and the soft crying of Elizabeth Hightower.

"He never would have seen the bluff in the snow," she sniffed. "He must have stepped right off—"

"He must have," Malone agreed. He said nothing about the mutilation of the body. David Chapel had most definitely been scalped. "Come on."

He led her away through the dusk, keeping her from the body, and as they walked back toward the shelter of the woods, he kept his hand clenched on his rifle, his eyes alert, sweeping the jumbled, empty land.

For it was not so empty as it seemed.

With the clear morning, the trail herd moved. Childes hollered out his orders, and the cowboys started the cattle ambling toward the mouth of Arapaho Canyon with whistles, shrieks, and yells.

The trail boss sided Camden Shoate, his eyes narrowing. "What the hell happened to your face?" Childes asked.

144

The man's eye was puffed shut and discolored to a shiny purple. His lip was split and swollen, his cheek split.

"Walked into a tree in the dark," Shoate answered.

"You sure?"

"I'm sure." Shoate wheeled his pony aside to work a cow back into the flank of the herd. Glancing around, Childes saw McBride whistling and waving his lariat, and he drifted that way.

As he expected, McBride's face was also battered, though not nearly as badly as Shoate's.

"Want something?" McBride asked casually.

"Nope. What happened to you? You walk into a tree too?"

"How'd you guess?"

"Seems to be a popular pastime on this crew." Childes rode silently beside Reb for a time. Eventually he asked, "Is it all over now?"

"What?"

"Damn it, don't play the fool with me, soldier! You know what I'm talking about. Is it over?"

Reb was silent for a long moment. He looked across the herd toward Shoate, then nodded slowly. "It's over," he said. Childes nodded with apparent satisfaction and turned his horse away.

Riding to the point, he found Windy and Jenkins.

"How's it look up ahead?" the foreman asked.

"Deep," Windy answered. "The first cows'll have a tough time of it, but I reckon we'll make it."

"Take a couple of the boys and use your horses to break a trail," Childes told Jenkins.

Jenkins touched his hat and peeled back. Windy nodded. "Now you're thinkin'."

"Hell," Childes said with a grin, "all Texans aren't dumb."

Jenkins and two of the cowboys passed them at a canter, and by the time the herd reached the canyon mouth, the three had trampled down a path between four-foot drifts. The herd leaders were reluctant to try it at first, but with a little encouragement they filed into the chute and out onto the wide prairie.

"I'll give you odds we make it by nightfall," Childes said to Mandalian.

"Nope. Won't take that bet. If you *don't* get this herd to the reservation by nightfall, you ain't much of a ramrod. Myself," Windy said, biting off a chaw of cut-plug, "I'm planning on seeing the agency tonight, Number Nine in the morning, and my chubby little squaw by afternoon. Don't disappoint me." He winked, and Childes laughed.

"Keep 'em movin', boys!" Childes called. "Man here's got an appointment that won't wait."

Pulling the wagon up out of the snow-filled coulee was a job. Lieutenant Taylor had his men tie on, but even with the extra horses and the straining of the oxen, the Littlefield wagon proved to be a load.

"You'll have to take some of your gear off, Littlefield," Taylor told him. "I'll have some men help you."

"All right." Cole Littlefield looked at his wagon, which rested precariously at a tilted angle halfway up the bluff of the coulee. It was snow over sand, and the wagon bogged down and slid two feet to the side for every foot it gained uphill.

With the aid of a couple of soldiers, Littlefield got to it, handing down three trunks, an iron stove, and various tools. A sack of seed corn followed, then a box of books. Forrester and Burns unstrapped the two water barrels, finding the contents of both frozen solid.

Charlie Burns felt the wagon tipping toward him, and he put his shoulder to it instantly, hollering to Forrester, "Damn it, have them haul tight on the lines over there. We'll lose the damn thing!"

Forrester, slipping and wading through the snow, ran to the far side and hollered to Stretch, "Keep that line tight, it's heeling over."

146

Stretch backed his horse, which itself slipped and slid a ways downhill in the uncertain footing. The line drew taut and the wagon settled on four wheels again.

Wiping his brow, Burns went to the back of the wagon, accepted a barrel from Cole Littlefield, and called in, "Don't you worry, Clarissa. Everything's under control."

"I feel like I should get up, Mr. Burns," she answered worriedly.

"Don't think of it! You just settle back and mind the baby."

Charlie turned, lowered the barrel, and saw Forrester grinning at him.

"What's so damned funny?"

"Nothin', Charlie."

"Well, quit that damned grinnin' and get to work."

"Yes, boss," Forrester answered mockingly. Still grinning, he transferred a crate to his own horse's back, tied it securely, and led the animal to the lip of the bluff.

Lieutenant Taylor was there when his horse, scrambling, achieved the rim of the coulee. "Everything all right down there, Private Forrester?"

"Fine as can be, sir. Mother Burns has taken charge." Forrester grinned again, and Taylor suppressed a smile of his own.

Burns waited for another crate, but Cole Littlefield told him, "That's all there is, Mr. Burns."

"All right." Burns stepped out from behind the wagon and waved to Lieutenant Taylor. "They'll try it again now. Lay easy, Clarissa. Nothin' to worry about."

The little girl sat wide-eyed, watching from her mother's side.

"Now, Cole, there's some weight you forgot. Come on, Linda." Burns waved at the Littlefields' daughter. "I'll give you a ride up."

Eagerly the little girl came forward, and Charlie stepped into the saddle. Cole Littlefield handed his daughter up to sit in front of Burns.

Charlie kneed his bay forward, and it scrambled up the slope, once going to its knees, sending snow flying. "Hold on!" he encouraged the girl. Then they were up and over and Charlie sat beside Taylor, watching the wagon.

Glancing over, Burns noticed Taylor smiling, carefully looking away, and muttered, "Wish I knew what in hell everybody finds so all-fired funny."

At Taylor's command, the soldiers tightened the tow lines and Littlefield whipped his oxen. The wagon seemed bogged down for a moment, but finally it moved. Heavily, awkwardly, it rolled up the slope, sunk to its axles in snow, the horses straining.

It tilted badly once, going over a hidden rock, and Burns's cry mingled with Taylor's sharp order. Looking sheepishly away, Burns mumbled, "Sorry, sir."

The wagon lumbered on and then was up and over, resting firmly on the flats. The lines were untied from the wagon, and Littlefield's goods were reloaded.

Charlie walked the little girl to the tailgate and lifted her up, but she clung to his neck.

"I'd rather ride with you, Mr. Burns," she said.

Charlie flushed, glanced at Cole Littlefield, and told Linda, "I'd like to have you, but it's army rules that you can't."

"Maybe we can do something about that."

Burns swiveled his head to see Taylor sitting behind him, hands crossed on his saddlebows.

"Sir?"

"He can't let you ride his horse, Linda," Taylor said, "but maybe I can let him ride up in the wagon box with you and your daddy. Kind of like a guard, if you want."

"Lieutenant—"

"Mr. Littlefield?"

"Fine by me, Lieutenant. I could do with the company."

"All right. That's settled." Taylor turned in his saddle. "Dobbs! Take Private Burns's horse in tow, will you?"

"Yes, sir," Dobbs called.

Burns stood there, the girl still wrapped around his neck, beaming. Silently he handed his reins to Dobbs and then he turned, clambering up into the box to join Cole Littlefield.

He was still seated there when, ten minutes later, Taylor moved his party forward onto the plains and toward Outpost Number Nine.

# *thirteen* ━━━━━━━━━━

The moon slid higher into the sky, casting blurred shadows across the snow beneath the pines. The silver moonlight caught the white of the land and glossed it. The land beyond the pines spread out in a shimmering blanket of silver and deep black. The high peaks, clothed in mantles of pure white, cut jagged silhouettes against the star-spattered sky.

She sat nearer to him, holding his arm. Malone had one arm around her; the other was free, and in that hand he held his rifle nearly as tightly as he held Elizabeth Hightower on that startlingly clear, awesomely beautiful, cold, cold night.

"I still don't understand why we can't have a fire," Elizabeth said.

"Wood around here's all too wet," Malone replied, his eyes fixed on the distances.

Elizabeth turned her head and glanced dubiously at the forest. She pulled the blanket tighter at her throat, looked up at Malone, and asked, "Have you always been a soldier, Malone?"

He shrugged. "No, not always."

She was silent, and he felt her shudder. Malone squeezed her arm tightly. The black trees swayed in the night breeze, and an owl cut a wavering silhouette across the face of the silver moon.

"Will you always *be* a soldier?" Elizabeth inquired. "I mean, have you thought of other occupations?"

"Most of the time I think about other occupations," he told her.

"But... have you seriously considered it?" She was serious, and Malone frowned a little. "Doing something else. Something better."

"Is there something better?" he asked, lifting an eyebrow.

"Many, many things." She paused thoughtfully. "You could be anything you want to. A doctor, a merchant—"

"Lion tamer, Indian chief."

"Oh!" She pushed away from him in exasperation. "How can I talk to you when you won't be serious?"

"I'll be serious."

"Promise?"

"Yes, I promise." He kissed the tip of her nose, finding it smooth and cold. He hugged her to him again. "Now just what is it you're aiming at?"

"Why do you think I'm suggesting anything?"

"Well, you're the first person who's had any interest in my choice of occupation since my Uncle Ike; he had a slaughterhouse and thought I ought to apprentice myself to him."

"And did you?" She sat and tugged him down beside her.

"I figured even soldierin' beat hitting a bunch of cows between the eyes with a sledgehammer."

"You know," she said after an interval, "there's an entire world you've never seen out there, Malone. The

152

way David and I—the way I live is probably unimaginable to you."

"Painting? Arty folks and friends. A—what is it?—manor house somewhere in England?"

"That." She nodded. "And so much more. Claret in the garden in the summer evenings. Fox hunting. Visits to the Continent—"

"What continent?" he interrupted.

"See! You can't be serious."

"I'll try again," he smiled.

"I have a lovely flat in Paris that I use three months of the year. And the use of a friend's home in Italy if I tire of winter. I travel the world, Malone, on a whim. I've done portraits of emperors, been given steamship passage and an exorbitant fee."

"I don't reckon I'd be much of a painter."

"I was thinking more of what kind of associate you would make."

"Associate?"

"A companion, if you will."

"Like a kept man?"

She was silent, nonplussed, her lips pursed. "That really is insulting, Malone. You've got to get over your rudeness."

"If I want to be kept?" he asked wryly. She pushed away from him and got to her feet. Malone rose to stand beside her, but she turned steadfastly away from him, watching the moon on snow, the chiaroscuro effect of moonlight and shadow, which her painter's eye appreciated.

Malone watched her face, profiled against the moon, and said quietly, "I'm sorry, Elizabeth, I purely am. But you know it's hard for me to take any of what you say serious."

She still did not look at him; arms folded beneath her breasts, she gazed toward the far mountains.

"You think I'm lying to you, Malone?"

"No. It ain't that. It's just that I know who I am. Or

153

I think I do. I've got no education— matter of fact, I don't think it would stick if I did have some."

"You could try," she said, some of the eagerness returning.

"I reckon." He shrugged and looked away himself. "But there's some men who just don't have what it takes to be a lawyer or whatever. Not that they ain't smart enough, but maybe they've seen too many phonies, too many folks with their noses in the air and their hands in other folks' pockets."

"We aren't all like that, Malone. Everyone who has a little money didn't get it by stealing it. I think I know what you mean, but have you ever thought that perhaps you are simply afraid to try, and this line of reasoning is an excuse?"

Elizabeth turned to him, her fingers going to his coat lapels, gripping them tightly as she turned those starlit eyes up to him.

"I have money, Malone. I could sponsor you, be your patron, and you could pay me back when you can."

"I'm sort of otherwise occupied right now," he said.

"Now, yes. But your enlistment will be up one day."

"Fourteen months." She stood on tiptoes and kissed him, almost roughly. "And then you will be free. Don't you see what kind of life we could have? Tramping across the countryside, making love, meeting a higher class of people, dressing well."

"And making love."

"Yes. Always that." She kissed him again.

"That would be after I got some of the rough edges off—I mean, I can't imagine you'd want me around your friends now."

"At any time," she said. Far away a wolf howled, and she trembled, closing her eyes. She leaned her head against his chest and it almost seemed real, all that she offered. Christ! What would McBride say?

"Sorry, Reb, I'm off to Old England to marry a lady of rank. I'd like to help you chaps pick up buffalo chips,

154

but Lady Hightower is expecting me in Paris."

And then Malone realized he had not been listening, not been fully alert. He had been thinking about rolling the lady in her manor bed, and not of the immediate situation. The moonlight fell brightly on them and the wolf howled again—only it was not a wolf.

Malone took Elizabeth's hand more roughly than he intended and said, "Come on. Let's get out of this light. Back in the trees!"

"Why, whatever—?" She started to laugh, thinking it was some sort of love game, but now she saw that he was deadly serious.

She followed him into the deep, concealing shadows, watching as he stood listening, the rifle in his hands. "I think we'd better travel on a ways," he said.

"Tonight? Are you joking?" She laughed and then became serious. Clutching his wrist, she asked, "Is it the wolves?"

"Wolves, hell. That's Cheyenne talk, lady."

"Cheyenne?" She shook her head. "I thought they were all placated. All kept on the reservations."

"Some are, some ain't. Some only are some of the time."

"That's very cleverly put, but—"

"Listen, there's no time for playing with words. Let's get a move on. They might have spotted us out on the slope. Likely did."

"But we don't have to worry tonight, do we, Malone? I mean everyone knows the Indians don't fight at night— something in their religion about losing their souls in the darkness."

"That's fine," Malone snapped. "You ever met any atheists?" She nodded, and he went on, "The Indians have their share of atheists too. Want to take a chance these renegades are religious?"

"No, of course not. But I mean"—she wiped the hair away from her face nervously—"how can you know they're renegades, as you call them, at all?"

155

"How? All right, I'll tell you. David Chapel had been scalped and had his fingers cut off. That's Cheyenne sign, lady. Now they likely know that we found Chapel's body. It could be these renegades were holed up here, hoping nobody would find them. There was a man called Blue Foot who dropped out of sight real sudden not long back. But now we've found them, and I just happen to be wearing an army uniform. They'll be right pleased to see that. Now let's quit jawing about it and get into motion, if you don't mind."

Malone knew he had been rough with her. She was trembling with fear. But there was no time for a pleasant discussion of the situation.

He felt sure the Cheyenne had spotted them and that that was the message the wolf calls were passing along. He also felt damned sure that to stay where they were would be to die, so they moved, and quickly.

Malone snatched up their pack and led the way through the moonlit forest. They waded down long, snowy slopes and across quick-running, icy rills. Once again they were into timber, deep and vast.

They were leaving a trail an Indian could follow at a run on this moon-bright night. But at least they would have to track them, to give pursuit, and not simply spring the trap Malone felt sure they had been planning.

They struggled up a long slope. Lady Hightower tripped and fell once to her knees, only to have Malone yank her up again. In the uncertain light, Malone went down himself over an unseen snag, banging his shin painfully. But they hurried on, twisting through the pines, the silver moon following them like a hunter.

Malone cursed it under his breath, thinking of all the preceding nights when the somber clouds had blotted out the sky.

They broke out of the forest onto a high, craggy ledge. The earth fell away sharply nearly five hundred feet. There was ice in the crevices, glinting in the silver moonlight, and, still distant, the snowy flats showed clearly at this altitude.

"Across that," Malone said, panting.

Elizabeth looked with dismay at the crown of ice-slick rock jutting from the mountain, and shook her head.

"I can't make it."

"You can. You will. They can't track over rock."

Elizabeth was bent over nearly double, trying to catch her breath. Running at this altitude was no easy matter. Not at night, after an already difficult day. But this— she felt that she could not make it, that she would just as soon let the Indians take her.

"Come on, dammit!" Malone barked, and he took her by the hand. She had no choice but to follow, and she did, cautiously, her heart pounding.

They moved out onto the bare rock, starkly silhouetted by the moon. The footing was slick, the rock uneven and icy. Elizabeth waved an arm and went down hard, bruising her hip. Malone yanked her to her feet and she whirled at him angrily.

"Are you mad? How do we even know they're back there?"

"I know," he said quietly. "And I know what they can do. Get moving."

He actually gave her a little shove to get her into motion, but she slogged on. They were on the bare rock for another five hundred yards. Then Malone veered off into the woods once again. The moon was sinking into the western mountains as they climbed the slope. It grew steep and difficult. They had to crawl along, tearing their hands on stone.

Ancient, wind-flagged pines stood starkly against the black mountain. Eventually they reached a teacup valley—a small, grassless depression ringed by trees, offering a view of the only possible approach to their position—and Malone nodded.

He sagged to the earth, his lungs fiery, and Elizabeth joined him, placing her head on his lap. Her breathing was tortured, her breast rising and falling rapidly. Her eyes were on him and she opened her mouth to speak, but couldn't find the wind to say whatever it was.

157

He put his arm around her, and her eyes closed. With one hand Malone yanked the blanket from their pack and covered her with it. The moon was nearly down; only a dull glow showed through the pines on the high ridge opposite them.

Malone pulled some dry, salty jerky from his pack and chewed it slowly as Elizabeth, her head on his lap, fell into an exhausted sleep.

Malone did not sleep. They were back there, and he felt certain they would follow. He sat there shivering, his rifle in his hand, his eyes searching the shadows as the night crept past.

"Sir?"

Captain Conway looked up at Ben Cohen, who stood in the doorway to his office. Behind Ben he could hear the sounds of sawing and hammering as the orderly room roof was repaired.

"What is it, Sergeant?"

"Telegram from Regiment, sir. They've got the line fixed now."

"Important?" Conway frowned as Cohen crossed the room holding the telegram.

"Confusing, sir, to say the least. Maybe it'll make more sense to you."

Conway took the telegram and tilted back in his chair, slowly reading the message, which, as Ben said, was confusing at the least.

"Malone!" Conway said, coming forward suddenly in his chair.

"Exactly my reaction, sir," Sergeant Cohen commiserated.

"Let me read this again." The captain shook his head.

FROM COL R E HAVERSHAM COMM FT
LARAMIE WYOMING TERR
TO CAPT WARNER CONWAY COMM OUTPOST
#9 WYOMING TERR

BRITISH SUBJECT LORD RUPERT MANNIX
HERE. DEPARTING IMM OUTPOST #9. REQ
YOU INFORM CHAPEL/ WHITTINGTON PARTY
REMAIN AT YR POST UNTIL MANNIX CAN
JOIN. PLS EXTEND THANKS PVT MALONE FOR
GUIDING PARTY THRU MEDICINE BOW
RANGE UNDER DIFF CIRCUMSTANCES.

REGARDS HAVERSHAM

Captain Conway put the telegram down on his desk, smoothing it with his fingertips. "Through the Medicine Bows? Damn, Sergeant, you know what it must have been like up there when the blizzard hit?"

"Fort Laramie seems to think they should have been here by now, sir. Does that indicate—?"

"It would seem to indicate that Malone and this Chapel-Whittington party are in serious trouble. Through the Medicine Bows! Good God, I wonder whose brilliant idea that was!"

Conway stood, looking at his wall map silently. Without turning around, he told Cohen, "Notify Lieutenant Kincaid, have him report to me."

"Yes, sir."

Cohen was gone with a snappy salute, and Conway again studied his map. If Malone and these Englishmen were caught up high when the blizzard hit, they had little chance of survival. Again he wondered what idiot had suggested taking the mountain route.

He would dispatch Kincaid and a search party, and he had little doubt that Matt would find them. But looking at that map, remembering that high country and the devastating blizzard, he held little hope of finding any of them alive.

# fourteen _____

She felt a hand on her shoulder and started to scream from out of her dream. Malone clamped a hand over her mouth before she could cry out, however. Sitting up stiffly in the gray predawn light, Elizabeth shook violently with the cold.

A low mist crept up the deep mountain valleys. There was ice on the trees and frost on the ground. Malone slowly removed his hand from her mouth and helped her to her feet.

"Let's go," he said in a low voice, and she nodded.

They could risk no fire for cooking, so they ate as they walked—dry, salty jerky and dry, salty biscuits.

They worked their way over the barren ridge and onto the timbered, northward-facing slopes. False dawn grayed the skies to the east, and the trees, which had been black shadows, took on form and texture.

They walked for two hours as the sun slowly rose, coloring the snowfields orange and deep purple, lighting the tips of the trees with gold.

Elizabeth stumbled time and again, but each time Malone hooked his hand under her arm and forced her to continue, to plod on until her legs became rubbery.

"I can't . . . I have to rest, Malone," she panted.

He looked carefully at her. "All right." The woman was exhausted. The past few days had been debilitating. If he didn't let her rest soon, he decided, he would be carrying her.

He found a small clearing where the sun touched the earth. There was a nearly square boulder in the center of it, and Malone swept the snow from it, helping Elizabeth to sit.

"You're cruel, Malone," she managed to pant. "God, I'm weary."

Still she managed a faint smile and Malone, bending over, kissed the dark crown of her head.

"I'll be off there a ways," Malone told her, and she gripped his hand tenaciously.

"Don't leave me!"

"I wouldn't. You know that." He smiled reassuringly. "I just want to have a quick look-see down the backtrail."

"Don't be long."

"I won't, I promise. You just rest up for a minute."

Releasing his hands, she leaned back, propping herself up with her arms. Malone wound his way through the trees, paralleling but not following their own trail.

Working his way toward an upthrust rocky crag, he began to climb. The exertion at this altitude was considerable, but he managed it. Fashioning a sling from his kerchief, he looped it over his shoulder and crept up the broken gray rock to the pinnacle.

Working forward on his belly, Malone searched the backtrail inch by inch. Nothing. He began again, sweeping the woods with his eyes. Maybe he had gotten himself worked up for nothing, but he didn't think so.

And then he did see them.

Five men, single file, jogging down the slope opposite

162

and a mile away from him. He got just a quick glimpse of them as they trotted across a clearing before reentering the woods.

It was just a glimpse, but it was enough. All five were Indians, all were carrying rifles. He had the impression that only the first two were Cheyenne, but he couldn't be sure.

He clambered down from the rock quickly and returned to where Elizabeth dozed away her weariness in the clearing. "It's time again."

"Can't we stay awhile, darling?" she asked sleepily.

"No, I think we'd better keep moving."

"You saw something?" She sat alert, reading something in the tone of his voice.

"I saw something," he admitted. There was little point in keeping the truth from her. "The way they're coming, they'll catch up quickly if we don't move. Probably they'll catch up anyway. We've got to find a place we can defend."

"Defend! You mean there will be a battle?" she asked, as if such things never occurred in the real world. Maybe in her world they didn't. Battles were only lines of print in newspapers, lists of casualties posted in the square.

In Malone's world they were pain, blood, the dead sprawled on the ground, the whoop of war cries, and the close explosion of rifles.

"Let's hope not," Malone answered. "Probably they'll give it up if it comes to that." His words were totally unconvincing.

These were renegades who had hidden far up in the mountains for crimes already committed. Now they had killed a white man, and a soldier had found the evidence. They knew that the army would not rest until they were rooted out and punished, and so they would fight. Fight to kill the witnesses to their crime.

They traveled on, again moving downslope, slipping and sliding on the treacherous footing provided by snow over pine needles.

163

The sun was on their backs, the snow a white mirror. Breath fogged out of Malone's mouth. Elizabeth moved like a marionette, lurching against him, legs wobbling, head lolling on her neck. Her mouth was open and she panted like a dog in summer.

"Really . . . really," she said, gripping his shoulders as they stopped before fording a narrow stream that bubbled past, singing across the riverbed stones. "This is too much! I simply can't—"

Her voice was broken off suddenly by the distinct, near crack of a rifle shot. Malone saw the bullet plow into the snow, heard a second report, and then saw a figure leaping through the woods, gesturing in their direction.

Malone brought his rifle to his shoulder and fired three times, missing high, then low, then to the left. The Indian was hot for the kill, but he was no fool. He dove to his face behind the trees, and Malone grabbed Elizabeth's hand.

"Come on!"

Her eyes were wild with panic, and she staggered after him. They splashed across the rill, heedless of the icy water that reached to their knees.

Another flurry of shots, all high, sounded as they raced for the concealing trees upslope. Those trees seemed far distant, and Malone half expected the searing pain of a bullet in his back at any moment.

But they made the woods. A last, searching bullet whined off the trunk of a massive lodgepole pine, tearing a chunk of the deep red bark away.

"Hurry," Malone urged Elizabeth. She moved on as if in a daze. They were fifty feet into the trees when Malone turned. The Indians, emboldened by their superior numbers, rushed headlong across the clearing toward the creek, yelping shrilly.

Malone went to a knee and fired. The Indian in the lead crumpled and tumbled headlong into the snow, his arms flung wide.

The others came to an abrupt halt. Two of the braves fired wild shots in Malone's general direction, then they all took to their heels, racing back toward the timber.

Malone settled the front sight of his Springfield on the back of one of them and squeezed off a shot. The round was low, tagging the Indian on the calf. He went down with a yelp of pain, got to his feet again, and scrambled toward the woods, limping badly.

Malone flipped open the trapdoor firing chamber of his Springfield, ejected the spent cartridge case, and reached into his pocket for another round. As he pulled it out and reloaded, he cursed softly; it was the last .45-70 round he possessed. He still had ammunition for his Schofield revolver, but he would lose the superior range and hitting power afforded by the Springfield, and he didn't relish the idea of having to deal with the Indians at close quarters.

He turned and snatched Elizabeth's hand again. They ran madly through the woods, dodging trees, leaping snags and rocks.

He did not think the Indians would quit. They would be more determined than ever, if anything. It would take them time to circle the clearing, but even now he knew the Indians were running through the forest exactly as he and Lady Hightower were—only a good deal more quickly.

Elizabeth gasped audibly and he felt her go down. She fell to the earth and he had to bend over, put her across his shoulder, and stagger on.

Suddenly an Indian loomed up in front of him, eyes slitted, rifle leveled. Malone fired instantly from the hip, and said, "Shit!" as he realized he had missed. Even as he dropped the rifle and clawed his Scoff from its holster, he berated himself for wasting his last rifle shot on such a close target. At that instant the Indian fired; the bullet whipped by so close to Malone's ear that he could feel its hot breath.

The Indian was obscured by powder smoke, but Ma-

165

lone fired anyway and heard a howl of pain, and as the breeze drifted the smoke away, Malone saw the Indian go to his knees, his face a mask of blood.

Malone turned sharply left and ducked into the brush. He ran on for a hundred feet, struggling under the weight of Lady Hightower. Then he stopped, crouching to listen.

Nothing. No footsteps, no crackling of the snow-heavy brush as a man moved through it. Malone was hardly reassured.

As quietly and as swiftly as possible he moved on, his temples hammering, his legs knotted. He came abruptly to a concealed wash and clambered down into it, twisting an ankle as a rock slid away from beneath his boot.

Looking up the ravine, Malone turned in the other direction, downslope. The going was easier here, where there was no brush growing, but Malone didn't kid himself. He was carrying double and he was beat.

Sooner or later the Indians would run him to the ground. His only object was to make it as late as possible.

He was nearly past the trail when he saw it.

Winding up through the scrub oak and manzanita was a nearly concealed game trail. It was steep and winding, leading to a rocky promontory that stood away from the mass of the mountain.

A huge yellowish outcropping, split by weather and by the two huge old oaks that tilted out from it, it offered a defensible position.

Malone's instinct was to run, but it was an instinct that he knew could get him killed. He opted for the rocks. Turning up the trail, he forced his way through the close tangle of brush.

Then, slowly, deliberately, he climbed toward the outcropping, Elizabeth's slight weight like that of a loaded freight wagon on his back. The wind lifted Malone's hair, tugged at his coat flaps. He half expected to be shot off that rocky slope, but he made it. Up and over and onto the wind-swept, bald crown of the stone tower.

166

There, panting, he set Elizabeth on her feet, watched as she sagged to a sitting posture, then crept to the edge of the rock.

In a minute they came. Three of them, single file down the wash, moving in an easy, loose-gaited trot. Malone drew back from the edge a little.

*Go on,* he thought, *right on by, men.* And for a moment he thought they would do just that. But these warriors had spent a lifetime tracking and they halted abruptly, glancing at the game trail.

Their eyes lifted toward the promontory and Malone fired, scattering them into the brush. Frantically he dug into his pack, finding the sack of ammunition for his pistol. Again he regretted the loss of his Springfield, but there was nothing to be done about that now.

Quickly he reloaded, glancing, as he did so, at the ravine below. Nothing moved, and he did not expect to see them again—until they made their final rush.

He felt Lady Hightower against him, felt her hand on his arm. Glancing at her, he saw those blue, blue eyes fixed on his face.

"Will they come?" she asked.

"They'll come."

"But you've shot two of them."

"That'll just give them more reason, I'm afraid." Aware of the panic in her eyes, he added, "Of course, it could be they'll take off. We've got position on them. No way up this rock without being seen." He attempted a smile and she responded weakly.

"God, what a place for my life to end. There were so many things I wanted to do yet. So much work yet to be completed."

"You won't die," Malone said.

"And if they capture me?" she gripped his arm even more tightly.

"Likely they'd ransom you to the army."

"I'm not a fool," Elizabeth told him. "And I well recall all those grisly tales you told us around the campfire."

167

Malone shrugged. "You never know what they'll do. But you won't die here. Not while I'm alive."

"I know that. We were fools, weren't we?"

"Yes, ma'am. I told you that way back. I tried to tell you that folks who are ignorant of this country have no business being here."

"I know you did. But we didn't listen, and look what it cost."

"It's an expensive education," Malone agreed.

"Terrible. David dead. And Charles. Those awful mountains, the blizzard, and now this! But I did meet you." The hand with which she had been gripping him now caressed his arm tenderly. "I won't forget you, no matter what happens. And you remember to tell them you're not reenlisting. We'll see Paris, Venice—"

Malone saw a quick movement in the brush, sighted, and fired.

He thought he had missed, but could not be sure. A rifle higher on the slope fired twice, and he ducked his head. A ricochet went whining off into the air, kicking up rock fragments that stung Malone's cheek and hands.

"They'll give up, won't they?" Elizabeth asked. She held his arm, her eyes closed, her forehead pressed against the stone.

"Sure. They'll give up," Malone lied.

Already he was thinking of moving. If a rifleman got up high enough on the peak opposite them, he would have a clear line of sight. It was quite a distance across the valley, perhaps half a mile. But given enough time and enough ammunition, they would be picked off eventually. And the rifleman who had fired at them was moving up.

Come dark, they would have to make a break for it. At dusk they would move and either live or die for it. Malone stretched out a hand and hugged Elizabeth to him.

She pressed close against his side, hugging him with desperate strength.

"Tell me about it," Malone urged her. "Tell me about Paris and how it will be living there. Tell me about this here Riviera."

And she did, speaking in a low, muffled voice. She spoke of distant lands, of people and events, forgetting for a time the danger of the present as Malone, half listening, watched the sun arc overhead and begin its slow descent toward the western mountains.

The shadows stretched out from beneath the trees, webbed, interlaced, and became dark pools. Malone stirred. Crawling back from the rim of the rock, he snatched the pack up and slung it around his neck and shoulder.

Elizabeth, who lay sprawled against the still-warm rock, peered up anxiously, and when she saw what Malone was doing she sat up, the cords in her throat taut, her eyes frantic.

"You're going!"

"Sh! *We're* going," Malone whispered. "I've been studying on it, and I think we can get down on the far side. It'll take some climbing, but I reckon we can make it."

"All right." She nodded obediently, but when he led her to the face of the rock and showed her what he meant, she gasped in terror.

"Malone, I can't," she said, backing away.

It was nearly a straight drop. A few tangled, brittle plants hung tenaciously to the rock, and there was a wide split that ran diagonally across the face of the cliff, but aside from these spare and tentative handholds, there was nothing to cling to, no place to plant a foot.

"You'll have to," he said sharply. "I can't carry you and we've got to go. You have to!"

She nodded mutely and hiked up her skirt, tucking it into her belt. Her pantaloons were absurd, white in the fading light.

"I'll go first." Malone started to turn, then came back. Holding her tightly, he stroked her hair. He kissed her, feeling the press of her pliant mouth against his, tasting the tears that had trickled down her cheek.

"Ready?" he asked.

"Yes." She smiled weakly and he nodded, moving away. Easing over the rim, he wedged his boot toe into the long crack, and holding a clump of dead brush, he eased on down.

His fingers sought holds, but found nearly nothing. Here and there a rough thumb of stone protruded, but the first one Malone tried his weight on broke free, nearly sending him tumbling to the earth far below.

He beckoned to a hesitant Elizabeth. She stood staring into the black depths, nervously fingering her face. Malone wanted to go now—now, before the moon rose.

"Come on," he said. "Then I can guide you. Do what you see me doing. Use the same handholds."

*Unless,* he thought wryly, *you see me fall. Then it'll be up to you, my lady.*

She got to her hands and knees and scooted over, her tiny boot searching for the crack. "A little to the left," Malone encouraged. "Atta girl. Over you come. There's a bush to the left of you."

Working that way, Malone finding a hold and then passing it on to Elizabeth, they made it down. It was touchy here and there. Elizabeth came within inches of falling, swaying wildly as she clutched for a handhold she could not find. But make it they did.

They stood together, panting, as the moon eased above the eastern horizon, illuminating the ravine floor like a beacon.

Now he knew the Indian posted high on the mountain would see that they had gone and send out the alarm. Even as he thought that, the sound of a wolf howling echoed down the long canyon, and the hairs on the back of Malone's neck stood up.

"Now we run," he said to Elizabeth. "Just run as far and as fast as we can. And it'll be all right. They're way behind us."

170

She fingered his sleeve and glanced once behind them. "All right." She nodded heavily. "I will run. You won't have to carry me this time, I promise."

"Good girl."

Malone looked into her moonlit eyes and then, grinning, gave her a last, lingering kiss. "You're a hell of a lady, Lady Hightower."

Then he turned, and with Elizabeth at his heels, he ran blindly through the night, racing away from a death that was so close behind he could nearly smell it. The pines were dark warlords in deep ranks along the high ridges, and the moon a searching torch. And somewhere behind them, the butchers also ran, and would run until Malone had been run to the ground, slaughtered, and left for the wolves.

# *fifteen* ———————

They ran until they could run no more, and then they walked, staggering, fighting for breath, for balance, for alertness in the numbing cold. They had come out of the mountains, but Malone was not sure they were any safer. The flat, snow-humped prairie gleamed in the moonlight. There was no place to run, no place to hide. Looking behind him constantly, he saw no one, however; and he had begun to hope.

It was a thin hope, drawn fine by the numbing hours, the interminable distances, the knowledge that he was outgunned and burdened with the woman.

He was exhausted at the hour before dawn, ready to lie down in the snow, to give up, to die. But Malone was not a man to give up, and if they wanted him dead, they would have to kill him themselves.

Dawn was a brilliant rose-colored explosion above the dark mountains. The snowfields were tinted red and then lavender, and the Indians came with the dawn.

"My God!" Elizabeth sagged to her knees, lifting a finger, and Malone turned that way, seeing the three widely separated figures.

He snapped a shot at them and they dropped to their bellies. "Come on!" he shouted.

"Where? Oh, God, Malone, they'll kill us!"

"Get up, dammit!"

An Indian, firing from the prone position, got off a close shot and Malone ducked reflexively, although the bullet was already well past him. He raised his pistol and returned the fire. Smoke rose lazily into the dawn sky from the Indian's rifle muzzle.

"Get up!" Malone hollered.

Finally he yanked her up and they ran through the snow, which was to midcalf, until it seemed there had never been a time when they had not been running, when the world had not been snow-covered, cold, and hostile.

Six rapid shots sounded behind them, and looking over his shoulder, Malone saw that the renegades were gaining rapidly.

The wind had risen with the dawn, and it was cold in his face. Hatless, the wind twisting his hair, Malone stood dueling-fashion and fired three times, once at each renegade.

Again they went to their bellies in the snow, and Malone reloaded rapidly, running on with Elizabeth, her face streaked with frozen tears beside him.

"There!" He lifted a hand suddenly. It wasn't much, but it was something. A long-dead tree, frosted with snow, lay against the flat expanse of prairie, and Malone turned that way, dragging the lady with him.

They leaped over the tree and pressed themselves to the snow behind it. A renegade's bullet slammed into the gray trunk of the dead tree, showering them with splinters, and Malone ducked.

Rolling over, he tore at his ammunition sack, finding only three brass-cased cartridges remaining. Cursing bitterly, he turned back to watch the renegades wriggling across the snow, occasionally rising up to fire.

When they did rise up, Malone took aim and fired, hoping to drive them back, but there was no stopping them now. Elizabeth lay beside him, and he could feel her heart drumming like a frightened rabbit's when he rested his hand on her back.

One of the renegades made a dash toward their position and Malone fired twice and watched the Indian tumble to the snow. Hit? He didn't think so. Now he could no longer see the others. Skilled guerrilla fighters, the renegades could use those low mounds of snow effectively.

Malone peered over the log, drawing a flurry of shots, six of them in rapid succession, causing him to pull back. As he did so, he knew that they would rush closer still.

Elizabeth was sobbing and he lay close to her, his arm around her. A renegade to his left darted a short distance and then dove to his belly, too quickly for Malone to respond. Another flurry of shots was cut loose. The bark of the dead tree jumped as each bullet impacted, and Malone ducked lower yet.

The air now was filled with light snow, and it puzzled him. The sky was clear overhead. He frowned and then heard a familiar sound, and frowned more deeply yet.

Horsemen. There were horses charging his position, their hooves picking up the snow, which the wind now blew over him. Malone heard another volley of shots from the renegades, and then a fusillade laid down behind him, and he felt his gut tighten.

He swung the gate of his revolver open, saw two unscored cartridges, and angrily slapped the gate shut. He rolled over protectively, face up, cocked weapon in his hands, Elizabeth beneath him, and he waited. The first two over that log would pay.

The shots increased, so near that black smoke drifted past Malone. Staccato rifle fire hammered at his ears. Elizabeth clutched at him, cringing from the day, the gunfire, the world.

A horse leaped the tree and Malone came up, holding his pistol with two hands, steadying it. He nearly fired before he saw the blue shirt.

The horse wheeled and Malone, sitting beside Elizabeth Hightower, slowly lowered his gun. Wojensky turned his horse and walked it to them. Leaning over, his hat tipped back, his rifle in his hands, Wojensky smiled.

"Some folks will do anything to get out of work."

Malone stood and looked around. Lieutenant Kincaid was riding toward them, and six soldiers were chasing down the renegades. Malone knew that a sheepish grin was spreading across his face, but it was uncontrollable. His legs trembled and he felt a hot tear coursing down his cheek.

Wojensky had dismounted. Walking to Malone, he threw his arms around him.

"Damn you, Corporal," Malone said, his voice breaking. "What in hell took you so long?"

Wojensky laughed and then Malone was laughing too, laughing until the tears fell from his eyes. He had to wipe them away to see Matt Kincaid. Malone managed a salute and an introduction.

"Lieutenant Kincaid, Lady Elizabeth Hightower."

"Lady Hightower." Matt touched his hatbrim and smiled, and Elizabeth, swaying on her feet, fell into his arms, clinging to Kincaid, who looked at Malone. Malone only shrugged.

"We'll take you to the outpost now," Matt said. "It's all over. A friend of yours will be arriving soon—a Lord Mannix."

"Rupert?" She touched her hair and stood dazed, staring into the distance. "I would like to see Rupert."

Matt disentangled himself from Elizabeth and walked to Malone, slapping him on the shoulder. "The others?" he asked, and Malone lifted his chin toward the distant, menacing Medicine Bow Range.

"Weather got 'em, sir."

Kincaid only nodded. Horses were brought forward and Elizabeth was helped into the saddle. Then they turned, with the renegades in tow, and swung slowly back toward Outpost Number Nine.

The orderly room door opened and Dutch Rothausen staggered through. He was whiskered, bruised, and haggard, but he was unbowed.

"I'm back, Cohen," he said gruffly.

"Dutch! Christ, man, where have you been? The captain's been worried about you."

"Yeah? Sorry. Weather held me up."

Cohen tried to read the expression in Dutch's eyes—an expression the big sergeant was trying mightily to conceal. He gave it up and nodded. "I'll tell the CO you're back."

"All right. I'll see you, I've got work to do."

"Tonight? Take it easy, Dutch. Let Farnsworth handle supper."

"Farnsworth! I'll tell you something, Ben, it's a wonder the whole outpost ain't down sick. I want that son of a bitch transferred. He'll never make a cook." Dutch turned and swung the door open roughly. Before going out he remarked, "Ben, I don't think the horses are treated well enough, do you?"

Then he was gone before Cohen could answer. Ben started to rise, then scratched his head with the stub of a pencil and shrugged.

Dutch stormed into the kitchen, and Farnsworth, holding a pot in his hands, recoiled.

"What the hell's going on here, Farnsworth? Think I wasn't coming back, did you?"

"Sarge, I—"

"Damn coffee pot's empty. What's the matter with you? Don't you know we got men working out in the cold? Is it too much to ask that there's coffee ready for them when they come off duty? What's that slop?"

177

He yanked the pot from Farnsworth, smelled it, and grimaced. "Clean me a big stew pot, soldier." Dutch turned toward the door. Walking out onto the plank walk, he threw the contents of Farnsworth's pot onto the ground.

"Hey, Dutch!"

It was MacArthur calling him, and Dutch was ready to chew the man out, reminding him that he was *Sergeant* Rothausen, but he never got the chance.

"Look!" MacArthur said, pointing to the main gate, and Dutch did look that way.

"I'll be damned!" the mess sergeant muttered.

In they rolled. Taylor leading his patrol, looking weary and dirty and cold. Dobbs was there, and Miller. Behind them came a civilian wagon.

A burly black man drove, and beside him on the seat sat Charlie Burns, holding a little black girl. Dutch blinked and shook his head. It was Burns, all right, and the kid was black as coal.

"I'll be forever damned," Dutch breathed.

He turned and, still shaking his head, went back into the messhall, roaring out orders. The door slammed behind him and MacArthur strolled toward the wagon, watching as Burns clambered down and Captain Conway emerged from his quarters to question and greet the party.

At that moment the Childes trail herd was rolling into the Indian agency. Dockery had ridden ahead, and with the assistance of two blanket-clad Indians, he opened the gates to the stock pen, and Childes' men and the soldiers hurrahed the weary steers home.

The Cheyenne emerged from their snowbound tipis, watching stoically. Children ran across the snow to perch on or clamber around the corral posts. Tom Hood, the most recent of the Indian agents to be posted to this forlorn agency, emerged from his house and strode quickly toward them, shouting his thanks to every man.

"Things were getting a little taut around here," Hood

told Gus Olsen. "I appreciate this—it can't have been easy getting through."

The cattle funneled into the corral with much bawling and clacking of horns, and when the last steer was inside, Childes himself swung the gate shut.

Then the trail boss and the Indian agent went off to settle up as the Indians appraised the gathered cattle. "Stretch the kinks out, men," Gus told his detachment. "We ride in half an hour."

McBride swung down stiffly and loosened his cinch. It was a moment before he noticed Camden Shoate beside him, his battered face apprehensive.

"Talk to you?" Shoate asked. He had his hat in his hands, Reb noticed. He shrugged.

"What is it?"

"You plannin' on turnin' me in for a deserter, McBride?"

McBride was thoughtful for a moment. Then shook his head. "I guess you're paying for it anyway."

Shoate looked at McBride and then beyond him toward the cattle, where a cowboy had let out an exuberant whoop. "I appreciate it." Shoate looked at the ground. "I don't reckon you'd shake my hand, Reb."

He extended it and McBride looked at the man. That sad, battered face, the pain behind the eyes. He was ready to refuse, but something prodded him to relieve the man of this small additional burden. *What the hell, it don't cost me anything,* he decided.

He took Shoate's hand briefly, and then watched as the man, shoulders bent, walked slowly away, leading his horse. Reb stood, hands on hips, for a long moment; then, out of some uncertain emotion, he kicked the snow, tugged down his hat, and strode back to join the other soldiers.

Windy was already mounted, sitting that long-legged appaloosa of his, and he barked, "What's holdin' things up, Olsen? Some folks got things to take care of, you know."

179

Gus grinned, wiped back his hair, and replaced his hat. "We got a man in a hurry," he called out. "Let's head it home."

Matt Kincaid led his party in shortly after four o'clock in the afternoon. Six troopers, three renegade prisoners, and a lady. Flora Conway was beside her husband as they welcomed Kincaid, and with much fussing and fretting she led Lady Hightower to their quarters, promising a hot bath and a strong cup of tea.

Malone slid from the saddle. Holding his reins, he watched Elizabeth go, noting that she did not give him so much as a backward glance.

He led his horse silently to the paddock, offering only a grunted response or a nod to questions and welcomes. He unsaddled and gave his horse over to the hostler. That done, he staggered back to the barracks and fell into his bunk, sleeping like the dead for hours.

When he awoke at last, it was with a ravening hunger. By the light under the barracks door, he knew it was morning and he sat up, feeling light-headed, stiff, and sore.

"Damn near time," McBride said. He was sitting on Holzer's bunk, facing Malone.

"Howdy, Corp."

"'Howdy, Corp,' your ass! Where in the hell have you been, Malone? That must have been some damn furlough."

"It was that, Reb." Malone rubbed his jaw. "It was that, indeed." He was silent for a minute, then he asked brightly, "Think Dutch would cook me up some eggs?"

"I know he would. Captain's orders. Seems you scored some big points, bringing the lady through."

"Did I?"

"That's what they say."

Malone rose, glanced at his beard-stubbled face in the mirror, and grimaced. He ran his tongue around his stale mouth and shook his head.

"Look like hell, don't I?"

"That you do," McBride said, rising to stand beside him. He handed Malone his hat. "Let's get you some grub."

The sunlight was piercing, the air cool as they stepped out onto the boardwalk. A fancy carriage and six civilian horses stood before the orderly room, and Malone regarded them questioningly. Seeing the curious look, McBride volunteered:

"Some English Lord, name of Rupert Mannix. He pulled in early this morning with his private little army."

"I see," Malone answered. The brim of his hat shaded his face, and Reb could not read his expression. "Let's eat, Reb. I'm starving."

Dutch laid it out for Malone, although he couldn't resist griping and moaning about special privileges. After six eggs, ham, and toast, washed down with three cups of dark, strong coffee, Malone felt almost alive again. He leaned back with a satisified sigh.

"Now all I need is a bath."

"You're not telling me anything I didn't know," Reb responded.

Together they walked out onto the plank walk, listening to the hammering of the blacksmith, the shouted commands as Miller put his squad through mounted drill. As they watched, the captain emerged from his quarters; beside him strode a tall, mustached man in a gray suit and gray hat.

"That's him," Reb said. "Lord Mannix."

Malone nodded. Six mounted men, armed to the teeth, flanked Lord Mannix's coach. Flora Conway appeared, and on her arm was Elizabeth Hightower, her hair arranged, face scrubbed, wearing a new blue silk dress.

As the two soldiers watched, the captain shook Mannix's hand. Mannix bowed stiffly, said something, and then moved to the coach. Elizabeth Hightower spoke to Flora and waved. Then Mannix helped her into the coach. He followed and shut the door.

Moments later the coach rolled past, and Malone saw

her for the last time. That dark hair glistened, and she smiled, but it was not for him. Those blue, blue eyes looked straight ahead, and then the coach with its armed escort was gone, rolling out onto the plains, where already there were patches of bare earth showing beneath the snow.

"Let's get on back," Reb said, slapping Malone's shoulder.

Malone stood there, watching the disappearing coach, lost in thought. Finally he nodded and fell in with McBride, and they strode back toward the barracks.

"They say she's a famous artist," McBride said.

"What?"

"Lady Hightower, they say she's a famous artist. Done portraits of emperors, lords, and ladies."

"And me," Malone commented quietly.

"You!" McBride laughed. "You mean to tell me she done you too, Malone?"

"Oh, she done me, son." Malone looked into the snowy distances, where the coach was only an indistinct smudge against the vast snow-covered expanse. "She done me good."

Watch for

## *EASY COMPANY AND THE LONG MARCHERS*

sixteenth novel in the exciting
EASY COMPANY series from Jove

*COMING IN MAY!*